THE STATE OF
CHRISTIANITY

DENNIS A. BEAUDRY

ISBN 979-8-88540-720-5 (paperback)
ISBN 979-8-88540-721-2 (digital)

Copyright © 2022 by Dennis A. Beaudry

All rights reserved. No part of this publication may be reproduced, distributed, or transmitted in any form or by any means, including photocopying, recording, or other electronic or mechanical methods without the prior written permission of the publisher. For permission requests, solicit the publisher via the address below.

Christian Faith Publishing
832 Park Avenue
Meadville, PA 16335
www.christianfaithpublishing.com

Printed in the United States of America

CHAPTER 1

Detroit

In the far-off distance, police sirens wailed, echoing among the man-made canyon of skyscrapers. The piercing, wailing cry soon faded, merging into the din of evening in the city. The long black shadows of the downtown buildings that had recently stretched eastward across the Detroit River now disappeared, blending into the darkness of the oncoming night. At countless places all around the city, an unknowingly unified army of people got themselves ready, anxiously preparing to venture into the murkiness of the nightlife. Some readied themselves for an evening of prostitution. Others headed out for a time of partying and reveling, while others made some final arrangements for conducting their illegal business by loading their Glock. Such was the case of a distinguished-looking gentleman in an expensive suit as he closed and locked a briefcase filled with several pounds of crack cocaine. Nighttime descends now on the city—Satan's premiere opportunity.

Not far from the concrete and asphalt of downtown, a small dingy white sign, with rotting posts and in desperate need of repair, stood in front of an inner-city church. The electric light on the sign hadn't worked since vandals smashed the glass and florescent tube nearly two years ago. The church building, likewise in disrepair, remained a place of worship for the faithful black congregation and their pastor. The Holy Ghost Baptist Assembly Church continued to stand in an archaic hope of being a beacon of light and life to the rapidly deteriorating neighborhood. Other than the sixty to sixty-five families that called the church home, there was just Pastor

Billy McPherson and his lovely wife, Ethel. Pastor Billy paused in his retreat to the parsonage, standing in front of the dilapidated sign, to once more read the note he had just posted with the aid of two thumbtacks.

> A very special church meeting, tomorrow night, 7 PM.
> Tell all the members you know and be here yourself.
> THIS IS THE MOST URGENT MEETING THIS CHURCH HAS HAD OR WILL HAVE PRIOR TO CHRIST'S RETURN!
> Our future and your future depends on your presence.
> Signed, Pastor Billy McPherson

Mabel Simpson, forty-six, was a lifelong member of Holy Ghost Baptist Assembly Church and had often seen the painful and tragic reality of the rampant drug abuse in her south side neighborhood. As bad as it had been in the early sixties, when marijuana had become popular, and as bad as it had gotten when the hallucinogens of the late sixties and early seventies made their appearance, still nothing could be compared to the current crack crisis Detroit was presently experiencing. Mabel could tell you of the increasing troubles that drugs just naturally attracted. She'd seen that sickening side of humanity over the years but had somehow been spared the personal experience—spared, that was, until three weeks ago when Ronnie, her sixteen-year-old son, was shot to death by drug dealers outside of her run-down house. Now she cried herself to sleep each night, half from the loss of Ronnie, half from fear of the thugs that roamed her street at night. She'd already decided to be at Pastor Billy's special meeting. For right now, though, prayer soothed her mind and spirit as she closed her eyes in search of rest and sleep.

Rufus Jones, sixty-eight, was a retired Chrysler autoworker. He lived four blocks east of HGBA Church and two streets north of Mabel's house. He served as an usher at the church and did whatever maintenance work he could, as far as keeping the building's plumbing, heating, and electricity working. Even at that, he was only partly successful. Three of the six toilets didn't work, and there was only one sink that operated properly. Rufus attended every service the church had and had remained faithful to his Lord Jesus since accepting Him as a child. He, too, had experienced the hideous, vulgar effects of a decaying neighborhood.

Two months ago, just after supper, several Detroit police cars and a vice squad van pulled up to the crumbling curb in front of his paint-blistered house. They were investigating reports of drug deals going on in the vacant boarded-up warehouse across the street. In a matter of seconds, several shots rang out, followed by an all-out life-and-death battle between the dealers and police. The barrage of bullets continued for nearly forty-five minutes. Then silence came, but not before three stray bullets found their way into Rufus's house. One came through a bedroom window, striking Rufus's eighteen-year-old unwed, pregnant granddaughter, Cloretta, in the shoulder. Fortunately, her wound wasn't serious, but he'd had enough! He'd be at Pastor Billy's meeting tomorrow night and be there ready for whatever happened.

Dr. Preston Jiles and his wife, Mary, operated a small family medical clinic five blocks west of HGBA Church. Three times in the past four months, their business has been broken into. A small amount of cash was missing after the first break-in. Police suspected someone was casing the office to determine if any marketable drugs were kept there. Apparently, while in the process, they stumbled upon the cashbox in the cupboard under the counter and hoisted it on their way out. The second and third times Dr. Jiles discovered there had been a break-in, drugs were missing from his small supply of pharmaceuticals, though he properly kept them under lock and key.

Barely able to keep up his malpractice insurance premiums, the three B and Es had resulted in higher property insurance as well. Mrs. Jiles was a registered nurse and for thirty years, had been employed by her husband, without pay for the past three years. She relinquished her salary because of the decreasing number of paying patients. Many of the families who used to call Doc Jiles their physician had left the declining area for what they hoped were safer neighborhoods. Now both in their late fifties, they had contemplated closing the practice and using what savings they have to move to Kansas, where Mary's sister, Charlene, lived. Although they had thought about moving, they hadn't made any specific plans yet—not long-range plans anyway. But they had determined to be at church tomorrow night to see what was so important.

Clifton Harris, thirty-three, was unemployed. He rented an upstairs room from Doris Filmont in another section of the rundown south side Detroit neighborhood. Plagued by a police record listing drug deals and possession of a controlled substance and having done fifteen of a twenty-four-month sentence at Jackson State Prison on those counts, he struggled through life as an ex-con trying desperately to make good. Clif went into prison a hardened black youth, forced by poverty and lack of education to resort to crime. He fit the typical police MO—trouble at home, trouble in school until quitting, gang association, and drunk and disorderly. The trail of his still young life was strewn with the evidence of countless misdemeanors, but things changed while he was doing time. He accepted Jesus as his savior and behaved himself for the duration of his incarceration, winning a parole nearly ten months early. He insisted there was no one single thing that led him to Jesus other than the cumulative effect and painful results of a reckless, godless existence. But having changed his heart and his mind, and prior to his release after earning parole, the warden had called him a model prisoner.

Since getting out, though, life had been tough. Although temporary part-time jobs helped keep body and soul together, he trusted his Lord to meet his needs, and thus far He had. Besides, Clif had been like a son to Doris, who was nearly blind. He read her the paper in the morning, the Bible at night. He helped with the housework and handiwork while meeting Doris's transportation needs, primarily to Doc Jiles's office, the grocery store, and, of course, to church—Holy Ghost Baptist Assembly—where they'd both be tomorrow night.

Fred Hampton, reporter for Action News, channel 8 TV, following a tip, pulled the station's highly visible van into a side lot near the police barricade that surrounded the Quick Place Party Store. Inside police officers were conducting the initial investigation of a robbery and homicide that had taken place just minutes earlier. No one was allowed in or out without police approval as they went about

THE STATE OF CHRISTIANITY

their business. Fred started taping his story in hopes of getting it wrapped up in time for the eleven-o'clock news. With his back to the scene, cameraman Tony Espoza gave him the go-ahead sign. Midway through the story, three shots and shattering glass pierced the cool damp night air. One officer was down, and so was the gunman. All the action was caught on tape by Tony for the eventual future police inquiry and trial. Apparently, one of those still at the scene had become a suspect during the course of the investigation, got jumpy, and started shooting his way out of the situation.

The wounded officer was Lowell Thorpe, head usher at HGBA Church, husband of Phyllis and father of Lowell Junior, John, Frank, Vincent, and Shary. The family was thankful that although Henry was in critical but stable condition at Henry Ford Hospital, he was expected to make it. Not so for the suspect. He died on the operating table two hours later. Lowell's family would be at church tomorrow night, not only for the meeting but to thank God for His mercy.

Pastor McPherson unlocked the front doors of the church about thirty minutes before the meeting. Ethel uncovered the organ and readied her sheet music. After turning on all the lights and checking the thermostat setting, Phil Demorest, elder, deacon, and assistant head usher, walked down the creaking tile floor to ask the pastor if there were any specific instructions for him to pass along to the other ushers as they arrived.

"No, Phil. This is strictly a meeting about the future of this church. We'll have Ethel play some hymns and then a season of prayer. After that it's strictly business, no offering, no bulletins."

Little by little the congregation arrived. About three minutes before seven, the church was as packed as a Sunday morning service. To Pastor Billy, it certainly looked like all his flock was there.

No time for a head count or roll call. They're either here, or they're not, he reasoned.

Ethel had called every household on the church membership directory.

The old organ popped, hummed, and rumbled in response to Ethel flipping the power switch. But soon her talented slender fingers touched each key the sheet music called for, and the congregation stood to sing "Amazing Grace." Several hymns in succession were sung as the reverent assembly made the transition from their flesh into the realm of the spirit. Pastor Billy stood up from his seat on the platform and walked slowly to the pulpit as Ethel lowered the volume of the organ and softly played another hymn as background music for her husband while he readied his notes. His flock remained standing, eagerly awaiting his next instruction. After motioning for his wife to stop playing altogether, he turned to the people and asked them to join him in a season of prayer.

"Our most holy heavenly Father, we humbly ask for Your presence here with us tonight. According to Your Word, 'Where two or three are gathered together in My name, I am there in the midst of them.'[1] Here we are, expecting You, Your Son, and the Holy Ghost. Bless us with wisdom and the words to express that wisdom to these, Your people, gathered here at Your instruction and my bidding. I know clearly what my spirit has received from You. There is no mistake about the direction You want us to take. I know it's Your power in us that we need in order to accomplish this immediate and most pressing task, as well as the long-range plan. We dare not do anything without You, for should we, we will surely fail. Prepare the ears and hearts of this people to receive the orders You've given me.

"Father, this world turns more and more in the direction of hell. You know that. We know that. You see that. We see that. Help us to take the course of action You will be directing in order to keep ourselves pure and holy before You. Deliver us, we ask, as Your servant Moses did the Hebrew children. Show us how to battle, where to battle, whom to battle, and when to battle. Don't lead us in a wilderness but rather bring us to Your promised land. Part again the sea, Father, only this time, not a sea of water but rather a sea of sin and worldly influence. Guide the steps of a righteous people. In Jesus's name, we pray. Amen and amen. You may be seated."

Every pew in the place, suffering from dryness and lack of proper treatment, creaked and moaned in response as the congregation returned to their seats. Pastor Billy slowly, without saying a word, looked smiling at each member as he walked staunchly down the center aisle. Every eye followed him. He stopped momentarily at the Thorpe family to console them and to tell them of his concern and prayers for Lowell's eventual recovery.

He reached the rear of the building, turned toward the front, and walked just as slowly back to the front, beginning to speak as he did.

"People," he started, "we are at a precipice here in our neighborhood. As you know, Detroit's crime and drug problems have significantly increased over the past ten years. I seriously doubt that one family represented here tonight has gone unscathed through this current epidemic of crime. We have felt its sickening presence. And we likewise know its source—the prince of darkness.

"I know I'm not telling you something you don't already know. I likewise won't be making some new deep revelation when I tell you that we still draw our strength from Jesus and from this body of believers, this church of our Lord Jesus Christ. But we have not been able to win, or even maintain our own, in the midst of this increasing darkness. I don't know why. God hasn't told me that. I wish He would, but He just hasn't. All I do know is that we, and the believers all across this city, aren't having much effect anymore on the society in which we live.

"As you know, Ethel and I have been contemplating a move to a new location. We've encountered a lot of spiritual unrest in that decision process, and now we know why. We're absolutely certain that that is not what the Lord wants because many of you wouldn't be able to attend any services should we move out of this neighborhood and leave all of you behind. Ethel and I wouldn't want you to live here anymore if this church, this sanctuary among the heathen, wasn't here for your edification. And we know if you can't leave, we can't either. That, in essence, brings me to the point of this meeting.

"Before I go any further, I want to preface the rest of my remarks with this: if at any time you feel uncomfortable about what I'm saying and you desire to leave, please do so. If at the end of this meeting, there's no one left in this sanctuary but Ethel and me, then we'll know and have release in our spirits to leave for a new church. But if you remain, joining us in the endeavor I'm about to bring to you from the Lord, then may we be blessed unto victory by Him that strengthens us.

"Friends, brothers and sisters in Christ, 'this is a hard saying, who can hear it?'[2] For the past seven months, I have found myself questioning God Himself and what it was He was trying to get me to receive and understand. His directions to me, throughout the course of my ministry, have always been very clear, very distinct, and very recognizable. That's why when He started telling me what I'm about to share with you, I found myself asking, 'Is that You, Lord?' Trust me. It was Him. Yet I didn't know why He was saying it or how I should go about telling you what He said."

"Preach it, brother! Tell us what He said," Clif yelled out.

"Please, Clif," Pastor Billy sternly retorted. "Hear me. This is important, maybe not fire and brimstone, but important just the same, for you, for me, for us, and eventually for America. The budget of this church is just barely adequate to make utility payments, some limited upkeep, and part of my salary. Those three things don't bother me as much as they used to. But it's going to get worse as family after family leaves the area. And too, the safety of this building is not getting any better. I've turned all that over to the Lord, probably more times than I can count. Each time I prayed about this, He kept bringing me to a scripture that had nothing—I mean absolutely nothing—to do with my prayer. That is, until seven months ago.

"Please turn to Romans 1:28–32 and follow along as I read. 'And even as they did not like to retain God in their knowledge, God gave them over to a debased mind, to do those things which are not fitting; being filled with all unrighteousness, sexual immorality, wickedness, covetousness, maliciousness; full of envy, murder, strife, deceit, evil-mindedness; they are whisperers, backbiters, haters of God, violent, proud, boasters, inventors of evil things, disobedient to parents, undiscerning, untrustworthy, unloving, unforgiving, unmerciful; who knowing the righteous judgment of God, that those who practice such things are deserving of death, not only do the same but also approve of those who practice them.'[3]

"Are we in agreement that pretty well describes this neighborhood, this city, this state, and even this nation?"

There came back from the pews a strong "Amen!"

"Would you agree that not-so-rosy picture depicts the world around us?"

A second chorus of "amens" came loud and strong.

"My brothers and sisters, would you also agree, that in prayers, in fasting, in our home life, church life, and day-to-day existence, we have tried to overcome these nightmares with little to no success?"

One more chorus of "amens" was heard, only this time with a twinge of sorrow and regret.

"Then lastly, my brothers and sisters, would you agree another plan of attack must be employed to be victorious in securing a life free from these dreaded influences and to defeat this city's enemy?"

"Amen and amen!" replied the people.

"Then, my brothers and sisters in the Lord, a new plan of attack it is. I was hoping you would be in agreement with me, but this plan has got to be bigger than just me. This plan that the Holy Ghost has breathed into me, as your pastor, is bigger than us as a congregation. This plan is bigger than five of the biggest churches in Detroit. The plan I'm about to share with you is even bigger than fifty churches. This plan has been given to several thousand churches simultaneously all across the nation. Yes, thousands of churches and hundreds of thousands of people who share in the desire to live above and not beneath. Yes, God had spoken to my spirit, but my head wanted to argue. I kept on fighting and hoping it might go away. But praise God, it didn't go away! Yet had I fought God any longer, He may have excluded me and excluded you because of me and my stubborn, argumentative spiritual ears.

"With your consent, tomorrow the church property goes up for sale. With your consent, we liquidate all the furnishings and supplies still on hand. With your consent, effective after Sunday night's service, I leave the paid position of pastor and work for you and the Lord, free of any further income. And with your consent, each of you and your families, start making plans to move with us to a new location."

"Where's that, Pastor?" someone yelled out.

"I don't know that yet. God's just told me to get you roused and ready. That's what I'm doing."

"Have you slipped a cog, Pastor?" came another voice from the otherwise silent crowd.

"No! Remember the scripture I just read? God's about to turn this neighborhood, indeed this city, state, and nation over to a reprobate mind. We're going to a new location, like Moses led the Israelites, like the pilgrims left England, and I suppose, like the Mormons went to Utah. To leave the place of bondage, to leave religious persecution, to look for a promised land, and, I suppose, to spare ourselves the wrath of God as did Lot and his family."

Three families, not able to discern the need to move, stood and left the church. The rest, eager for more instruction, remained to hear more.

Two hours later, the Johnsons sat at their kitchen table having an evening snack and conducting a family discussion. The topic was the special service held earlier by Pastor McPherson. All four members of the Johnson family were present: Clarence, his wife, Ruth, and their two teenage children—Balinda, seventeen, and Clarence Junior, fifteen.

Mr. Johnson rested his hand on top of the Bible, as it lay opened at the book of Exodus. They had started with prayer the discussion that slowly revealed how the call from God would affect their lives. Balinda was first to acknowledge the move would cost her the long-held dreams and plans of her recently started senior year in high school, dreams that included her third-year letter in varsity cheerleading. It would also alter her college plans and could even jeopardize her grade point average and thus scholarship possibilities.

Clarence himself, a pipe fitter for nearly thirty years, would have to surrender his present good-paying job, in order to start again someplace else, but, he reckoned, the call of God never gets truly answered cheaply. He told the children how he was struggling with turning loose all that he and Ruth had built together but knew that the Bible said all these things "will melt away with fervent heat"[4] someday. That verse helped him put things into proper perspective.

THE STATE OF CHRISTIANITY

Ruth had been serving as leader of the weekday woman's Bible study and prayer group for more years than she cared to count, but she figured that was just a preparation time for her spirit. Drawing close to God, as she put it, allowed one the opportunity to hear better. That's what she was doing now, after listening to Pastor McPherson—hearing better. Besides, if all the families moved, she reasoned, she may very well be able to continue in her calling at their new location, maybe even while en route.

Clarence Junior wasn't so sure. During the past few years, he had shown evidence of wavering in the faith of his childhood. Reaching those trying teen years hadn't helped matters any. The worldly influence of neighborhood friends and school associates had taken the wind out of his spiritual sails. For years, as a youngster, he had been a member of the children's choir. He had eagerly accepted, when asked, to sing Christmas and Easter solos. God had blessed him with a beautiful voice, yet of late, he seemed to be drifting away from God and church. His friends had lots of money from their secret drug deals and petty larcenies. Clarence managed on the meager income from working at the corner grocery store. His friends seemed popular with the girls; Clarence wasn't because he felt uncomfortable doing the things they did, and it showed. His friends had plenty of time to party and roam the neighborhood; Clarence had to work. Everywhere he turned, Christianity seemed to leave him socially on the outside, looking in. Starting all over in a new place, making new friends, wondering if he would even be accepted by others, just didn't appeal to him. Not at all!

Clarence and Ruth could see the results of the decision. They didn't want to state it out loud, but the fact remained. Choosing God, choosing His direction, might very well split the family up—three against one, one against three. Three would be taken; one would be left. They took comfort in those paraphrased scriptures. They seemed to verify the expected results of such a choice, knowing other families might also be sharing similar grief.

The two held hands across the table, praying for their son and all the sons and daughters and families of their congregation. Meanwhile, Satan hovered over the Detroit skyline and sneered at

Clarence and Ruth's prayer as it ascended heavenward. Suddenly, though, his expression changed to that of raucous glee. The prince of hell began to laugh loudly and mockingly at the couple's prayer, which he considered to be an anemic and futile effort in light of his influence and the chaos running rampant in the city. Satan had his plan, but he didn't know the extent of God's plan. Neither did the Johnsons—they couldn't for it was bigger than their imagination. Satan was further handicapped in that he didn't know the future. After all, even he knew that the future was God's domain—and God's alone. The prince of the air couldn't even begin to see what was about to happen on the West Coast.

CHAPTER 2

San Francisco

"I had a text and sermon already prepared on Friday, but for some unknown reason, I felt compelled to turn once more to the Lord for His guidance. He knows, and you know too, I'm not one to change directions abruptly, except when He directs by His Spirit. I know I look tired. It's because I didn't sleep much last night. In fact, I didn't sleep at all, as my wife, Lorrain, can attest."

The independent congregation sat attentive to their senior pastor, Howard Schmidt who was not known for extemporaneous homilies but rather for following prepared outlines. To be sure, he had always attributed his sermons to the promptings and leadings of the Holy Spirit, but not in such an impromptu manner as today. Something was noticeably different this morning, both in verbal intensity and mannerisms. Even his wife looked anxiously at him from the front pew. If anyone on the face of the earth knew Howard, it was she. For over twenty-six years of married life, two years of missionary work in Brazil, and three years of engagement while in seminary, she had watched, listened, and learned about this man of God she lovingly and loyally called her husband. Lorrain could tell he was now displaying a side of his personality, a quality that wasn't or hadn't normally been his.

"You see," he continued, "there are at least three churches on this side of the bay that have received a special anointing for an end-time purging, a shaking if you will, of the church of Jesus Christ. We are one of them. I know some of you are going to receive with eagerness both the knowledge of and the ability to demonstrate this anointing, while others won't be able to receive it at all. Most of you will go home after this morning's service and discuss, in great detail, with your noon meal what you are about to hear. That's good! Be sure to do that. This special anointing is God's way of getting 'a chosen people, a royal priesthood, a holy nation, God's special possession, that you may declare the praises of him who called you out of darkness into his wonderful light.'[5] To paraphrase it, a people set apart.

"We know God has said we are in the world but not of it. And we know that He has warned us not to even look like the world, in our lifestyle, in the way we do business, in the way we conduct ourselves. But I believe the call to be different, to be separate, is getting even stronger and more demanding. The call is becoming even more dramatically obvious. Certainly, the call is getting more challenging. The revelation is to separate ourselves from among them, even as was done in the Old Testament by the nation Israel.

"Sin is as rampant in this city as it was in the days of Sodom and Gomorrah. It's not even a new sin. It's the same sin. We can't help but see it openly, blatantly, and defiantly each day as we go about life. The evidence of it is on your left and on your right. The billboards unabashedly proclaim it, the world's music defiantly resounds it, the movie industry seductively projects it, and television's double entendres escape the broadcaster's code of decency. Try starting a day without noticing it. I dare you to time it to see how long it takes for this sin, or any sin, to raise its ugly head each day. Don't think for a minute you can even read the Sunday newspapers—Satan has his influence there too! I'm not trying to make something new out of yesterday's headlines. Simply and painfully clear to those of us who try to keep ourselves unstained by it, is the fact that we are living in a sinful and perverse nation! And it gets worse every day. Closer to home, we're living in a sinful and perverse city! God cannot be pleased with what He sees. Trust me, He's not! And what's more, He's about ready to pour out His wrath. Look closely, and you can see His work of preparation.

"Try looking at this nation from the perspective of God's eyes. If you were God, would you continue to allow us to enjoy the freedom we have today? How about the peace we have come to take for granted in light of the troubles and terrorism the world experiences? Would you continue to bless this land with the bounty it has? Of course not. There's been warning after warning. Look at the calamity and malaise that has come upon this nation over recent years. Look at our position or status in the world today. Once so great and powerful, where are we now? See how the warning signs come—more and more rapid they come: skirmishes and shortages, finances and factions, demonstrations and division. Look at the warnings that have come from so many of the faithful pulpits across the land. We nearly lull ourselves to sleep, lying to ourselves, saying it can't get much worse, yet it does. The heathen won't listen. Should we even expect them to? The government doesn't care. It really doesn't know how to care anymore. And the public sits in its own self-righteous complacency.

"But we, the church of the Lord Jesus, can no longer just sit on its hands! Especially those churches, such as ours, who are being called and given the opportunity to remain after the shaking of God. Those churches, such as ours, who are hearing the alarm from Zion. Those churches, such as ours, who are being readied to move from this place and into the land God has prepared for us."

Frank Morris, a senior executive officer for a downtown San Francisco company, leaned over to whisper in his wife's ear, "I can't follow him. Can you?"

Marriane Morris smiled and replied, "Why, sure I do. He's giving us directions from God. We're moving out! Just exactly where, I can't say. I sure hope he tells us it's a literal move, not a spiritual one. But whatever or wherever, we are moving out!"

"You might be, but I'm not! I've got a good job here. I won't leave all that I've worked for to follow some crackpot preacher trying to pull a 'Jim Jones' look-alike move on us."

"Shh!" someone from behind noised. Frank turned around snarling, then exited the pew and the church, lighting up a cigarette the moment he got through the door.

John Simms, assistant pastor, walked slowly across the platform and stood beside his boss. He'd been hearing rumblings in his spirit for several months now, ever since their petition drive to the city manager and mayor failed to prevent some legislation from being passed. At the heart of the legislation was the tax-exempt status of church properties belonging to denominations or individual churches that take anti-homosexual stands. That petition drive garnered nearly thirteen thousand signatures just from the section of the bay area they were responsible for. In less than forty-five days, the enacted ordinance would revoke the tax-exempt status of Jesus, the Redeemer Church, and many others across the city.

"Did you have something to say, John?" the pastor asked.

"Yes, sir, if I may."

"Please do."

"Thank you, Pastor Schmidt. Members of Jesus, the Redeemer Church, listen please to what you are hearing here today. This is the start of the next move of God, if not for the world, certainly for this nation. I have been hesitant the last three months to talk to the pastor about what God has been revealing to me, only because I didn't know exactly what it was. Now I know and the revelation that Pastor Schmidt is bringing to you today is that very same thing I have been hearing.

"There are many churches across this city who have joined together to find the God-centered way to confront the homosexual situation within legal constraints. Not from a condemning spirit, not from a hateful or vengeful slant, but rather from the same kind of heart that Jesus Himself has toward them. He wants to save them, but they aren't interested. Instead of submitting to His authority, they're intent on forcing their agenda upon the rest of the population. God has had enough. Although we read in His Word and know by experience that His mercy endures forever, we also see the results of His wrath throughout the Bible. When God has had enough, believe me, He's had enough!

"Let me give you the crux of what God has been showing me. But before I do, let me explain why I've waited to reveal it until now. I not only sought God for a deeper understanding of what He was revealing, not only confirmation upon confirmation did I request of Him, but I waited until I was certain our pastor had the same vision, the same leading and prompting of the Holy Spirit. Apparently, we've had the same promptings all along but did not voice them to each other, hoping we would yet hesitant to be the one to start the dialogue.

"I don't aspire to put words in our pastor's mouth. He's quite capable of speaking his own spirit. But God has shown me that we are on the verge of taking our boldest of steps with Him that we shall ever take on this planet. Don't just hear him. Please listen as Pastor Schmidt continues to show you what God has shown to us."

Pastor Schmidt returned to the pulpit, nodding in agreement to John, and then started, "People, you have just seen the Spirit of God in action. Seeing as how we've gone this far with God, let us continue.

"Legislation will not work. Even the critics themselves say that we can't legislate morality. I daresay we can't even get it on the floor of the state house for a vote. Our critics, those who oppose our Christian values and morals, yell 'separation of church and state' each time we speak out on a topic that crosses a political line that they themselves have drawn. Those political lines are becoming more and more vague as social changes and mores plummet to all-time lows. Certainly, we've all heard and can remember the poignant question 'Isn't anything sacred anymore?' America has resoundingly answered, 'No!'

"We've tried petitions. We've taken our stand from the pulpit. We've joined pickets and other demonstrations, under the guidelines of the law—all to no avail. And so now God is calling for drastic action to be taken! He wants to bless this nation again, but it refuses to bend its knee. It refuses to confess His Son's name. America wants no part of God and as such, has turned not only a deaf ear but its back on God as well. Arise, church of the living God! Arise! Our next move is a move!"

"They shouldn't have been in this area. What were they thinking?" Officer Duane Capole, forty-seven, San Francisco Police Department asked no one in particular. The Cambridge Street Apartments had a pitiful reputation for every vice known to man, and now here was even more evidence of this housing project's decay. He stood there with his notepad in his hand, gazing at the three bloody bodies, nude, facedown on a grimy mattress. Although autopsy reports would be the ultimate authority for cause of death, it was apparent the three, two males and one female, died of multiple stab wounds. Continuing his investigation into the homicides, Officer Capole learned the three were "religious freaks," as some had described them, from that Redeemer Church down the street. It was well known for its street-witnessing programs among the homosexuals and drug addicts.

"Hello! God bless you. Can I help you?" came Lucetta Gonzales's response to the two police officers standing in front of her receptionist's desk at Jesus, the Redeemer Church.

"Yes, ma'am, we would like to talk to your senior pastor, let's see, Howard Schmidt. Would that be possible now?"

"I'm certain it would be. Please have a seat while I check with him."

Officer Capole and his assistant, Tim Lawrence, sat quietly as their eyes did a complete scan of the small but efficient office. There was nothing out of the ordinary here. Just the standard church stuff—soft Christian music in the background, pictures of Jesus on the walls, and a large cross on the wall above the magazine table stationed between the two chairs they sat in. The magazine titles were the typical kind one would expect to find, all having a Christian theme.

After about three minutes, Pastor Schmidt arrived, introduced himself, and escorted the two policemen into his study.

"I suppose you're here investigating the murders," the pastor spoke.

"You're right, Reverend," came Capole's terse reply. "What can you tell me about the three? Where all three members of your church?"

"Yes, but it's the Lord's church, not mine. David Southern, Paul Grimes, and Terri Brandt. All three were members here, part of our street-witnessing team. What else do you need to know about them?"

"Anything you know about them, anything at all that might be important in our investigation."

THE STATE OF CHRISTIANITY

"Ahhh...let's see...maybe I ought to consult their files... Lucetta," he said into the intercom. "Could you bring me those three folders? Ahh, yes, here we are. David was twenty-seven. Paul, nineteen. And Terri was twenty-two. David and Terri were married, not to each other, but Paul was single."

"Pastor, just why were they in that building? Didn't they know that's trouble for sure?"

"Of course, they knew the trouble in that sector. They'd been briefed and trained for proper service on our teams. That's why they were there. And that's why they were there in a team, to try to keep this kind of thing from happening. Have you got any leads? Do you know who did this awful thing?"

"No, sir. But we know from the autopsy they were raped, sodomized, beaten, and then stabbed several times each. We can't tell yet where it happened. We're just not certain if it happened where we found them or not. Tell me about your street-witnessing program, you know, the one they were doing."

"It's really quite simple. The teams have their assigned areas of responsibility. They go with specific instructions to stay out of buildings, witnessing only to those they encounter on the street. They have a supply of things to hand out to those who are in need, things like food and toiletries, along with some tracts and Bibles. Their job is to tell others about Jesus and the plan of salvation. It's not any different from any other street-witnessing mission program at other churches. Nothing unique about it to the human eye, but there is a difference to the spirit."

"Explain, Pastor."

"Well, we believe in the empowering presence of the Holy Spirit. He gives us the knowledge, power, and ability to do this task of love."

"Excuse me if I don't buy that intangible religious stuff, Reverend. The bottom line is your people were out there where they shouldn't have been. They were in direct violation of last year's city ordinance restricting religious activities on the streets and sidewalks. My god, Pastor, remember the trouble we had a year and a half ago with the fanatic Power of the Mind group? That's why we have the new ordinance! They were there at your knowledge and direction!

We have a warrant here for your arrest. The charge is endangerment. Tim, read him his rights."

*****

Assistant Pastor Simms addressed the Wednesday night crowd, knowing he was talking to the core of that body of believers, Spirit-filled people who would be able to understand. The midweek service started with prayer as usual, but it seemed to be deeper, more intent, and last much longer than normal. Everyone knew of Pastor Schmidt's arrest and now prayed for his release. The air was energized with a deep prayerful intensity that seemed to illuminate the church on its own. After forty minutes of intercession, John approached the pulpit.

"Brothers and sisters, I have visited with the pastor in jail. He sends his love your way. He wishes he could be here, but they've not set bail yet. He's not certain he can make it even if they do. And he feels it would be a waste of money at this point. But he does send some instructions to us, in light of what transpired in the Sunday morning service and yesterday over in the Cambridge Street apartments. Let me read his letter to you.

"'Fellow followers of Christ. Let us continue to prepare for our exodus. Don't concern yourself for my situation. It is a minor one and shall be remedied by the Lord Himself. Soon, I hope. Until all things are resolved, spend your energies in prayer, fasting, and preparing for our move. The Holy Spirit has shown me much in the past several hours of incarceration. This will be a move of faith, but let us not think we differ from the Hebrew nation that followed Moses. It may be the early years of a new century, but we are no different. Our circumstances appear different only on the surface. Let's compare.

"'The Hebrews were under a heavy weight—theirs being slavery to build Pharaoh's monuments. While we tend not to think of ourselves as slaves, except to Christ, we are under the weight of a sickening, decaying, and crumbling society. The Hebrew people were from another land. So are we. They needed a new home. So do we. They were trusting in their God. So are we. They were praying to their God. So are we. They heard the instructions of their God-appointed leader, Moses. So are we as we listen to the Holy Spirit. And they were obedient to move when the time was right, making all necessary preparations as instructed. So shall we.

"'People be prepared, be ready, get your shoes on. This is not a spiritual allegory. Get ready to leave this city. God has a place for us to go to, prepared and waiting for our arrival.'"

John looked intently at the congregation, pausing long enough to study their facial expressions. "Friends, and especially our bereaved friends, hear the words of our pastor. We are going to be led on a divine pilgrimage to a land that is to be given unto us when we enter into it. This will be too extreme for some, and the extreme situation calls out for help from our God. Do you believe He is able to supply the kind of help and guidance this extreme case requires? If you are truly in tune with your spirit and to the prompting of the Holy Spirit, then this will not seem so extreme. Obedience is our only choice for survival."

*****

Robert and Frances Howland applauded robustly as their only child, June, now nearly twenty-two, crossed the stage. She had performed her ballet moves exquisitely, both the compulsory and free expressive style dance routines. The recital was the final phase of the competition that would catapult three young ladies and two young men to the point in their dance careers they longed for—an invitation to perform and tour with the San Francisco Balletmet, with pay for two seasons. June had geared her entire high school and college educations around seeking such an opportunity—indeed, her entire life, dancing since her preschool days and competitively since junior high.

She was tall, graceful, and yet light in weight. The majority of her height came from two slender yet muscular legs that were so well trained they could do the required routines while her mind dwelt on the prize she aspired to. Her face radiated pride with charm as she crossed the stage to receive one of the five invitations. She had finished first, and a future in dance was now assured.

As her mom and dad applauded, they looked at each other with the kind of pride only parents can beam when their child garners such successes, yet in spite of the unfolding accolades being presented to their daughter, they knew it might all come to naught should the call of God, through the ministry of their pastor, Howard Schmidt, rouse them from the moment and quicken them for a move from the city they'd come to call home.

Bob leaned over to whisper into his wife's ear as the applause quieted momentarily between the announcement of winning names. "You know, Fran, it's going to be just like this when the rapture comes. We'll be doing things in life just like day-to-day living. We'll be going about our normal routines and looking forward to Christmas or vacation or paying off the mortgage or some other upcoming event. The only difference is we won't have the privilege of an advance warning as we do now."

"Yes, I know, dear. That's the part that hurts a little. After the rapture, we won't care what we missed out on or left behind. We'll be seeing the glory of our Lord, gazing upon His precious face. But this time is different. Not so much for us. We've lived a good deal of our lives, but for June. I'm so glad she knows, serves, and loves the Lord. It gives me peace in my heart knowing she's already chosen Jesus and His call over the temporary joys of this life. But it would still be nice if she got in a few months with the troupe. I wonder where He'll call us."

*****

In spite of God's unfolding drama across the nation, Satan carefully calculated what he felt were to be his next offensive moves. He was certain that God was being forced to respond to him and his dirty work, and that pleased him, yet something gnawed at him. He ran to and fro across the country looking for an opportunity to influence man, manipulate the circumstances, and ravage the plan of God. His search stopped momentarily in New Orleans, Louisiana. Something caught his eye. The small wrecking crew he had placed there years before and that had been supplemented by reinforcements of late had been quite successful and virtually unchallenged in wreaking their havoc. The demonic influences had infiltrated and nearly captured the entire city unawares. All, that is, except for a small pocket of resistance fighters protected and urged onward by their heavenly Father. Satan landed in the crescent city to inspect his troops and size up the future confrontation. He quickly discovered that all was not going as well as he thought. Even Satan, fussing and fuming at what he found, admitted to himself that this was a nightmare in the making of dynamic proportions.

CHAPTER 3

New Orleans

Faith Community Fellowship was a church with a mixed congregation. In fact, it was about as mixed as one could get. There were Hispanics, blacks, whites, Cajuns, Indians, rich, poor, middle class, English speaking, French speaking, and even some of those back swamp folks who were the only ones who knew what it was they spoke. The building was just outside the southern city limits and not in an especially good section of town. However, it wasn't the building that drew this diverse group of Christians together, but rather was the dynamic little Holy Ghost-filled pastor affectionately known as Brother Domi J. Felice. Actually, that was short for *Dominique Jacques Felice*. This was his fifth church. Domi had started all four of the previous churches—one in Corpus Christi, Texas; one in Texas City, near Galveston; one was in Lake Charles; and the one prior to Faith Community Fellowship was in Gulfport, Mississippi.

At each of these churches, he had taught and trained up a Pentecostal body of believers who would start confronting the social decay of the cities where they were located. So it was with Faith Community. The express purpose of this growing congregation was to stir up the citizens' awareness to the evil and sin that ran rampant in the streets of New Orleans.

Most people immediately think of the Mardi Gras as soon as they hear the name New Orleans. Parades, parties, festivals, doubloons, jazz music, "When the Saints Go Marching In," bazaars, drunken brawls, sickening perversion, prostitution, homosexuals, transvestites, lesbians—all those things had become an accepted

THE STATE OF CHRISTIANITY

part of life in the city at the mouth of the mighty Mississippi River. Regrettably, over the years, the indulgent reveling had grown from a few festive gala celebration days prior to entering the Lenten season, to a 365-day a year notorious, obnoxious, rabble-rousing boisterous lifestyle. Initially conceived by and tolerated too long by the religious community, it was now deeply entrenched and thriving as an uncontrollable frolic by the king of hell, Satan.

As Brother Domi had often said, "This city has got a hellion runnin' loose, and he ainta goin' go down easy like. We goin' fight him tho, and he goin' know what it is that hit him too—the power of the almighty God Himself."

Evidence of the sinful lifestyles and declining moral standards were everywhere. Elder Charles Pointeaux, suspected to be anywhere from seventy-five to nearly ninety years of age, spent most of his life on the shrimp boats that scour the coast of Louisiana, Texas, and Mississippi. He joined on with a shrimping crew at the age of eight, staying with it until he could afford a boat of his own.

Now retired, he would tell the younger folks at the church of a time when "the automobile was getten' real popular and there was a gas station on each corner in New Orleans. Sometimes there would be two or three on them more busier street corners. Now, though," he would update the story, "we got bars, whorehouses, adult bookstores—sells you stuff that sends you straight to hell. They even got places now where they…well, I better not say. There's young ones here who don't need to know the sins of this city yet.

"One time, a few years back, I had just gotten in from three straight days shrimpin'. We'd run 'em for a while then drift with the tide, then run 'em agin. Well, the ice was about gone, so we came back in to sell. When we had gotten ashore, we wanted to get a bite to eat, you know, somethin' better than what we had on the boat—dry sandwiches and stale pretzels. It was some time ago 'cause I was nearly ready to retire. Just wantin' to get the season done and back home to Ma. We stopped in this place that we always used to go to for gumbo. It had the best in town. It was a place, happened to be just remodeled, you could bring the whole family. But this time, I and my partner, Jim DeSales, was in there orderin' our gumbo when this real pretty woman came up to us and sat herself down, right in the booth with us. First, she looked right. Then she looked left. Next, she looked over her shoulder and into that booth right behind her. By this time, we were a wonderin' if she had somebody after her and wantin' to hurt her. Then she leaned over to Jim, slipped her hand under the table, and grabbed Jim right in the private area.

"At first, I didn't know what she had done, but then she started talkin', and we could tell, sure 'nough, that this was no lady. Her voice was soft but deep like a man's. We was so surprised to find out the restaurant was done sold to somebody else, and he turned it into a place that people go who want to be somethin' they're not.

"It's just gettin' worse and worse. People who love the Lord, who want to stay sure of themselves with Him, goin' to have a real hard time to do that. Not so much for me. I strengthened myself over the years, keepin' in the Good Book. Those kinda things don't tempt me. I really don't know how they could tempt anyone, but they do. But the younger Christians, the 'babes' as 1 Peter 2:2 calls 'em, they goin' to have a hard struggle to keep themselves set apart. What really needs to be done is to teach all the Christians in this country how to get baptized in the Holy Ghost. Without His indwellin' presence, there ain't no flesh goin' to stand against this wickedness that's takin' over the country, and especially here in New Orleans."

*****

Brother Domi sat in the center chair in front of the Sunday evening crowd of about three hundred. To his left was Elder Charles, and to his right was Elder Jerald Cummings. Elder Cummings was a rotund black man, forty-eight years of age. He used to play tackle for a small northern Louisiana college football team but found himself involved in prostitution in New Orleans and Shreveport. He wasn't a big-timer in the prostitution rings; he was merely a travel agent, as they were called. It was his job to transport hookers that were released by the Shreveport police to New Orleans and vice versa. This procedure kept the police guessing for a while because the girls' names never jived with fingerprints and mug shots.

If Jerald had stuck with just driving the limousines back and forth, he would have been okay, but after learning the route and what the bosses expected, he'd find time to stop off in towns along the way, such as Coushatta, Colfax, Pineville, and Bunkie, to make deals with the girls for himself. Soon he was as hooked on sex and perversion as the clients the girls routinely saw in the two big cities.

While in a motel with several of his transports, the state police raided their room. All were arrested, and Jerald soon found himself on the receiving end of swift justice. Now an ex-con with no real skill other than that of an itinerant construction site worker, he scraped out his living picking up scrap lumber and other building debris and litter and then properly disposing of it. He also suffered from a lingering, uncorrectable venereal disease, which not only rendered him sterile but single and lonely.

The prison chaplain that counseled with him eventually led him to the Lord. That was nearly twenty years ago, and he's been on fire for God ever since. It was his personal testimony five years ago at a camp meeting that resulted in over fifty youth coming to the Lord at the first altar call. His strong faith, coupled with that testimony, has had similar results in many churches and youth camps across southern Louisiana, Mississippi, and as far away as Mobile, Alabama.

He cautioned the teens he encountered to avoid the trap that society seemed to be laying for its young people. "Don't use your sexuality as a toy or a growing-up experiment. Once you make it dirty, it's soiled for life."

The offering was being taken up as Samantha White sang an up-tempo toe-tapping rendition of an old hymn that soon had the people on their feet, clapping in time with the music. Afterward, Elder Charles started a time of prayer for the sick of the congregation, the unsaved of the city, and the convicting Holy Spirit to fall upon the nation. Then Brother Domi, in his slow, methodical style, approached the pulpit, adjusted the chrome gooseneck microphone holder, and cleared his throat.

"Hallelujah, are you blessed by the almighty God? Then tell Him so with an offerin' of praise and worship!

"Now then, if you feel you must, be seated to hear the instruction of our God. Before I give you the scripture passage we goin' to use today, let me tell you this is goin' to be some different kind of day. 'Why,' you might ask. Okay, I tell you first, then we read God's Word. If you been hearin' God in these services the past several months and if you been listenin' to God in your private time with Him each day and if you remember the things I told you about the four other churches God built and let me be a part of, then you know God been gettin' His people ready for action. But God slipped somethin' new in His message lately. We been hearin' through prophecy that we also supposed to be gettin' ready for movin' into a new land.

"I must not been listenin' too good or God been talkin' kinda soft to me. I thought He meant some kinda spiritual land, maybe new spiritual ground He goin' to start showin' us. But He showed me it's about time to move literally, and not just me. All of you supposed to be goin' too. You might as well say 'amen' 'cause if you don't go along, you goin' to be outta God's will, and that's no place to be, and one more thin'. This isn't an afternoon picnic either, so be packin' more than a Coke and two shrimp po'boy sandwiches. Now for the scripture. Are you ready? Then let's go!

"Brother Mike Orson, from the choir, is goin' to come and read the scriptures as you turn to follow in Isaiah 35. Go ahead whenever you're ready, Brother Mike."

"Father God, anoint these words recorded in Your Holy Word. They are life unto us, for without them we surely will die.

"'The wilderness and the solitary place shall be glad for them, And the desert shall rejoice, and blossom as the rose; It shall blossom abundantly and rejoice, even with joy and singing. The glory of Lebanon shall be given to it, The excellence of Carmel and Sharon. They shall see the glory of the Lord, The excellency of our God. Strengthen the weak hands, and make firm the feeble knees, Say to those who are fearful-hearted, Be strong, do not fear! Behold, your God will come with vengeance. With the recompense of God; He will come and save you. Then the eyes of the blind shall be opened, And the ears of the deaf shall be unstopped. Then the lame shall leap like a deer, And the tongue of the dumb sing. For waters shall burst forth in the wilderness, And streams in the desert. The parched ground shall become a pool, And the thirsty land springs of water; In the habitation of jackals, where each lay, there shall be grass with reeds and rushes. A highway shall be there, and a road, and it shall be called the Highway of Holiness. The unclean shall not pass over it, but it shall be for others. Whoever walks the road, although a fool, shall not go astray. No lion shall be there, nor any ravenous beast shall go up on it; It shall not be found there. But the redeemed shall walk there, And the ransomed of the Lord shall return, and come to Zion with singing, With everlasting joy on their heads. They shall obtain joy and gladness, and sorrow and sighing shall flee away.'"[6]

"Thank you, Brother Mike. Those words were spoken prophetically to the Jewish people, but they can also speak to us. We are told that God's mercy endureth forever. My personal belief is that promise is for those who accept God's mercy in the first place through the shed blood of Jesus. Obviously, in Noah's days, God's mercy didn't endure forever, for eventually he brought a flood. Too, in the days of Lot, God's mercy was directed toward His elect, not the sinful population of Sodom, as fire and brimstone hailed down on that perverse generation. And look at how God made His people victorious over tremendous odds as they purged the promised land of the tribes and kingdoms that were there. All in an effort to rid the land of sinful and idolatrous influences.

"Now let me ask you a thought-provokin' question. Why, just why, did God need to clear out the other people and kings so dramatically from the land that the Jewish nation was goin' to be given? Let that question roll around inside you for a minute.

"The reasons are many. Some of them are spelled out in the Bible. One of those reasons was, as I just said, to keep the Jews free from the idolatry of those people that were there. God knew if He let some of the occupants survive, they would continue their pagan practices and thus have a possible influence, over time, on the Hebrews.

"Now let me ask you a more up-to-date series of questions. Don't be raisin' your hands or answerin' out loud, just be answerin' internally. How many here occasionally play the lottery? How many here have a television and sometimes watch somethin' you know violates the Word of God? Is there anybody here who partakes of a little wine, beer, or other alcoholic beverage? Have you ever found yourself lookin' at somethin' that triggered an impure thought? I'm almost sure that there might be one or two of you in a congregation this size that smoked a cigarette on the way to church this evenin'. There may even be someone who did some kind of illegal drug sometime this past week.

"Do you see the point I'm tryin' to make? We may not like to admit it, but we, too, are like the Old Testament Jews—we can be influenced by the practices of them people around us. Now to be sure, some of those thin's may be residuals from our pre-born again days, but the total victory isn't there as long as the trigger mechanisms are constantly bombardin' our senses. That's why God told us to watch what our eyes see, what our ears hear, what our hands touch, what our mouth speaks, where our feet take us, what our minds think. That's why He tells us to keep ourselves separated from the thin's of this world.

"Well, I've said all that to get to this point. We been doin' a pretty pathetic job of keepin' ourselves separated. We been doin' a terrible job of bein' the holy nation that God wants us to be. We ain't been too bright a light in the midst of the dark and troubled world. We haven't been the salt that the world needs. They ain't too many beatin' the doors on this old church down to git in and git saved. But don't be too hard on yourself. We all have freedom of choice. Is it our fault we have freely chosen to sin? Maybe it's not totally our fault. The influence of the world, specifically this nation, hasn't been all that conducive to livin' a life that's pure and holy. How can we be what we're supposed to be when so much of the dirt that we pass through each day gets on us and dulls the brightness of our witness? In a nation that's goin' to hell as fast as time will allow, we can't seem to get their attention, let alone try to persuade them of the folly of their way and the certainty of the judgment of God to come.

"Now we know we can't convict the world of its sin if we look hypocritical to them. If they can see we speak with 'forked tongue,' they'll let us know that in an instant. They'll be sure to tell us when they smell somethin' rotten in our testimony versus our actions.

"'Well fine, Brother Domi,' you might say, 'How can we be the best witness, convict the livin' daylights out of them, and still be livin' in this world?' Well, I can tell you we've been tryin' and makin' very little headway at it. Some might say we been a losin' ground. But God's got the win already won, so it's up to Him to show us how to secure it for us. It's not goin' to be as easy as fastin' a couple of days a week. It's not goin' to be a prayer conference or even an evangelistic or healin' meetin'. What it's goin' to take is somethin' real drastic when compared to the attempts of the past two hundred-plus years this nation been takin' to get in the miserable shape it's in.

"We just goin' to have to be available to hear, obedient to employ, and be immediate in response to the urgency of the call. We goin' to get ready to leave this city, and I'm not talkin' the rapture! I'm talkin' gettin' in our cars, vans, motor homes and leave whatever we have to behind. If you're committed to the Lord and you hear His call, then don't just get ready. Be ready!"

A large chorus of cheers and amens echoed out the doors and down the hallways of the church building. Nearly all seemed to receive the instruction to prepare. Nearly all.

Lou Demmers didn't. He bit his lip and sat quietly until the service was over. When Brother Domi dismissed the people, Lou inched his way forward to the front against the tide of people going in the opposite direction. Soon he stood at Brother Domi's side, waiting for him to finish talking with an elderly lady.

"Hey, Lou," the pastor started, "what's on your mind tonight?"

"Well, I listened real good to all you had to say tonight. And I thought back to the past several weeks of services, and up till now I haven't had any trouble with what you've been saying to us—that is, until tonight. What about that 'greater is He who is in you than he who is in the world'?[7] You seem to be sidestepping that part of the Gospel in order to pull something off here that don't sit too well with me. Can you explain?"

"Lou, my dear brother Lou. You don't think I would come before the sheep God entrusted to me this way if it weren't Him directin' me, do you?"

"Quite frankly, I don't know what to think."

"Well, let me assure you that what has happened here tonight hasn't changed the validity of the scripture you just referred to. We still got the Greater One livin' inside us, but bear in mind that doesn't change the nature of our package. We still got this flesh wrapped around a whole lot of spiritual strength. It's that outer wrappin' that keeps gettin' soiled, like I mentioned earlier tonight. It's that outer wrappin' that stops the unsaved from seein' the truth of our changed spiritual state. Wouldn't you agree that Satan has stepped up his attack?"

"Yeah, I'd agree with that."

"Do you think that's caught God unprepared?"

"No, that just couldn't happen!"

"Then do you think God has to move against Satan the way you think He should?"

"Of course not, Brother Domi. Just where you trying to lead me?"

"Just to this. God always has His countermoves to offset anythin' the devil has tried to do. Just because we never seen God work a particular way before, certainly doesn't negate the possibility of God doin' somethin' new, or at the very least, something new to us. That's what He's doin' now—somethin' new, just for us, just for this time. I personally believe—and bear in mind He hasn't shown me everythin' yet, just the call to get ready—that we will be pullin' up stakes and going somewhere here in America that will be ours and ours alone. Somewhere where we won't get our testimony tarnished. Trust God, Lou. Trust God! He still has it all under His control, and He always will."

"I know that. I just hope you're hearing is okay, spiritually that is."

*****

Reginald Sheffield celebrated his thirty-third birthday last Friday with family from out of town and several of his closest friends. Now just days later, and after mulling over for at least the fifth time the words of his pastor, Brother Domi, he turned out the light in his small office. As he sat in the darkened room, he pondered the course his life had taken over the years. He contemplated his Methodist background and how a rift had developed between him and his parents when he first told them he was about to leave the family church years ago while living in Memphis. He didn't intend it to cause such heartache for them, but he did what he knew was the Spirit's prompting. Since then, the longing of his heart had been relieved by his own personal Pentecost.

On Sunday, he persuaded his visiting family to accompany him to the evening service before their return flight to Tennessee. That might have been a mistake, he thought to himself. It opened deep wounds again and brought ill feelings back to life. Things had been said once again that would have been better left unsaid. They left in a huff, evidence that they were still dissatisfied with his choice of, as they put it, radical emotionalism instead of good old-fashioned religion. Brother Domi's sermon didn't help matters either—talking about moving out and all.

Reggie's thoughts then turned to his one lone dream, indelibly a part of him as far back as he could remember. A dream inspired by a childhood visit to New Orleans, a dream to have his own art gallery in the French Quarter. He couldn't draw a straight line or even a good crooked one. Though art was his life's passion, his attempts in school had achieved nothing higher than passing grades. He was no artist, and he knew it, but he knew art when he saw it.

The evening was getting late. He had closed and locked the door to his four-room art display. Although the shop could be described as nothing more than a hole-in-the-wall, the location was great, and his dream was now a reality, a reality for better than four years now. In fact, his shop, which only displayed works of local artists, including oils, pastels, sculptures, as well as photography, had earned a reputation for having superb exhibits portraying some of New Orleans' best new and undiscovered artists. After a financially difficult first year, the profits of the past three had proven to him that the gallery, the French Quarter Louver, could support him.

Reggie propped his feet up on his backroom desk, breathing a short prayer for guidance. "Lord, sometimes I wonder about the times in which You decided I should be born and live here on planet Earth. At times, I wish I were part of a different generation. Preferably a past generation, considering how this world is going. Then You do something real significant in my life to make me realize these are exciting times. As the clock moves relentlessly forward, Your Holy Spirit is at work within the church Your Son is building, here and around the world. And, too, we get closer and closer to His soon return. But, God, the sin that surrounds us, the rampant sin that surrounds us, sometimes overwhelms us in our efforts to stay clean while we live our lives here.

"I know You have all things under Your control, yet I see the times in which I live and long for a quieter, gentler nation. You have been so good to me. Look at the success You have blessed me with, only because You love me, not because of what I've done for You. Father, I surrender all this back to You, asking only one thing in return. Please keep me in Your plan and purpose. Include me in Your next outpouring. Make sure I'm a part of Your next move. I'm ready, Lord, to leave this all behind, be it around the world or just a mile down the street, so long as it's a mile closer to You and Your kingdom."

*****

The Evil One lingered in the dark alley behind the art shop listening to Reggie as he prayed. *This pathetic and simple man typifies the weakness of my enemy,* he thought. *He will be easy to discourage, but then why should I dirty my hands on such a small project? I'll dispatch several of my flunkies here to keep the family discord festering and maybe cause a fiery disruption to this insignificant's life. However, they must be careful that they do not harm the bar and strip joint next door. I still need them and their business. But as for me,* he continued, *I must see what is happening with my cause in New York. There are rumblings up there I do not recognize.*

CHAPTER 4

New York City

A crowd of nearly eight thousand stood silently across the street from the Women's Health and Guidance Center in the heart of New York City. They had been there nearly ten hours, all holding signs that depicted a developing child inside an embryonic sac. The vigil was illegal, but they weren't concerned about the consequences. They were standing in the gap for the unborn who had nothing more for their defense than their silent cries that went unheard and unheeded by the now boisterous crowd on the other side of the street.

The opposing forces wanted confrontation. That was obvious. They ranted, raved, screamed, catcalled, and jeered at the pro-life gathering. Over the hours, the scene had deteriorated to this near-volatile point. The government didn't want to get involved but found itself thrust into the courts by both sides. The elected officials and other authorities had become noncommittal, afraid to say anything. The most they would say was, "Let each state decide for itself what code it might deem appropriate for the people within its boundaries." Actually, that stance didn't set well with either side. Each was afraid the other would gain the upper hand and force their wishes upon the rest. What they really wanted was a decisive and formidable law to be enacted. Because of the government's hesitancy, the verbal hostilities had escalated to confrontational levels across the nation in hundreds, possibly thousands of cities and towns.

The pro-choice side demanded legalized abortion at any time during the pregnancy. Pro-lifers desired protection for the unborn children. It had started in 1973 and grew to its present capricious apex by the many state and federal Supreme Court decisions that expanded abortion rights. Court case after court case had murderously gone in favor of the pro-choice faction, pushing the nation deeper and deeper into a holocaust of hellish proportions.

Even when medical science broke the DNA code, no change came to the seared conscience of the nation. When scientists had researched further to find the previously unknown DNA character quarks, similar to atomic quarks, there was no corresponding change in society's stand on the issue. Some of those in the medical world would cautiously call the newest DNA findings "viable life determining factors," announcing the existence of VLDFs found to exist in embryos within the first thirty seconds of fertilization. Proof of the finding had been recorded with computer-enhanced microscopic videotaping procedures, yet other doctors and scientists discounted the discovery and maliciously continued to do their financially lucrative evacuations, with no concern for the fledgling life.

New York had, during the past several years, become the center for the antiabortion cause. That may have been due to the increasing number of procedures done there as compared to the rest of the nation, or it could have been the sizable group of protesters that gathered there during a recent national rally. Whatever the reason, this band of protesters had braved a chilling evening and two torrential downpours with severe lightning. Forming up at midnight, the group swelled through the predawn hours to the point where morning rush-hour traffic was snarled to a standstill and pedestrian traffic could barely move at all.

Emotions and demonstration tactics of the nearly five thousand in the pro-abortion camp were getting uglier by the minute. Police acted as a buffer between the two, receiving jeers of the pro-choice side for not arresting all the pro-lifers.

The spokesman and leader of the pro-life group, Reverend Theodore (Ted) Arsley, whose church accounted for only three hundred of the gathering, grabbed the bullhorn and climbed the steps of the makeshift platform on the back of a flatbed truck. He had a prepared statement ready to read publicly and fully intended to do so when apprehended by the Spirit of God. His nervously trembling hand hung at his side, holding the bullhorn. He lifted his eyes to heaven and breathed a short prayer for strength, wisdom, and guidance.

Slowly and deliberately, he raised the bullhorn to his mouth while his eyes scanned both sides of the street and the swelling crowds. "People of this city and the nation, the murdering of innocents has gone on long enough! We won't tolerate it any longer. We have petitioned and prayed. We have had courtroom date after courtroom date, with defeats at almost every turn. We have called for legislation and gotten none. We have voted our consciences for representatives, governors, and presidents but have had only minimal impact on stopping this atrocity. We have blockaded clinics such as the one across the street with few successes and many setbacks. God is not happy with the results of our frail, meager, human attempts to stop this tragedy. He expects more. He demands more! He has enabled, empowered, and equipped us for a speedier and more dramatic demonstration against this hideous crime. Once more, like Moses going to Pharaoh, He is commissioning us for action of a different kind. A demonstration of His making that will not only get the attention of those who advocate abortion but literally stop them in their murderous tracks.

"It is not confrontation that I speak of. It is not arguing or debating. It is not a slick public relations ploy. What it is, is a step of faith in our God to deliver not only these precious unborn children from the hands of the heathen and their self-serving practice, but to deliver us as well from His wrath, rightly poised to fall upon this land for the iniquity of abortion. *Abortion*, the ugliness of that word and the insidiousness of the act, plagues and pulls this once-great nation down. People, hear me! We have a most ambitious thing to do. Not a well-intentioned repetition of futile, weak efforts of the past, but rather a more auspicious gathering of His warriors, ordained, anointed and destined for victory, orchestrated by God Himself to serve as a final warning to this country and, indeed, the world.

"I entreat you to return to your homes now! Pray! Seek God and attend services this Sunday where God's direction will be revealed to large and small congregations alike. At that time, at countless assemblies across this city, we will be given instructions for this mighty move of God. Let the opposition be warned! You are going to see the indisputable blessing of God come to this side of this noble conflict. He will demonstrate to you, visible even to your blinded eyes, the error of your ways and the power of his deliverance."

"Okay, mister. You want to come with me? You are under arrest for inciting a riot. Please come peacefully. It'll go better for you if you do. I think you've said enough to put you away for a while. We have it all on tape. Anything you say can and will be used against you in a court of law. You have the right to remain silent—"

"Officer, I know my rights. Thank You, Jesus, that I can suffer this persecution for Your name's sake, for great is my reward in heaven. You said, 'Let the little children come to Me,'[8] As a little child, I come to You now, trusting You and placing all my faith in You, asking for deliverance, strength, and patience as I await Your help."

"Okay, folks, this illegal gathering is now concluded. Go home now or be arrested like your leader here. Go on! Leave this area now!"

Reverend Ted was handcuffed and led away under a ten-man escort to the arrest wagon three blocks away. As they escorted him away from the platform, the crowd started dispersing, many praying softly in English while others prayed in a spiritual language.

"Excuse me, Reverend, but I must do this. First, empty your pockets and put all the contents on the counter, where it will be inventoried. Thank you for complying. Now raise your arms and spread your legs. I need to search you for any hidden weapon or other contraband. I know it's difficult in a moving vehicle like this, but I need you to take off your pants and put on this jail suit. Your shirt too, please."

*****

Deacon Jeff Kamister stood in the pulpit left vacant by Pastor Ted's arrest. He had, on occasion, found it necessary to address the body of believers that called Roush Road Trinity Church their spiritual home. Even then, when the pastor was at a revival elsewhere, on vacation, or filling in for a sick pastor at neighboring churches, Jeff would nervously hold services for the flock. All the people looked up to this saintly thirty-eight-year-old deacon. He was the youngest deacon they'd ever elected to that position, but God had gently spoken to them to do so, and they obeyed.

Jeff was single and had dedicated his life long ago to serving the Lord, though never prompted to go to seminary or get ordained. He seemed content with the direction God had led him, that being to open a small Christian bookstore. That was over fourteen years ago. What had started with a small business loan had now matured into a million-dollar facility and twice that amount in stock. Now the business was flourishing from not only local business but a large lucrative web-based mail order clientele as well.

Today, though, he had the always humbling and awesome task of filling in for his activist pastor who, for his stance against abortion, was on his third day of a fifteen-day jail term. Deacon Kamister asked the congregation to turn their Bibles to Philippians 2:15.

He waited for the shuffling pages to cease and then started reading. "'That ye may be blameless and harmless, the sons of God, without rebuke, in the midst of a crooked and perverse nation, among whom ye shine as lights in the world.'[9]

"Saints of God, so long as we apply the whole armor of God, abide in His love, rest in His salvation, trust in His Word, and obey His commands, then we are indeed blameless sons of God, without rebuke, in the midst of a crooked and perverse nation. Our Light—that is, the Lord Jesus who is the Light of the world—shines brightly as He never has before in our day. That's because against a background that grows increasingly darker, light can't help but shine brighter. Yes, our light shines, both individually and corporately, yet the world, the darkness of the world, if you prefer, comprehends it not. That's because it is deliberately choosing darkness and blindness to an obvious light.

"Why doesn't the world comprehend our light or the light of Jesus Christ? Think along this line. Our sun is really a star, a close star, a mere ninety-three million miles away from us—close in comparison to the next nearest star. It is bright to us because of that closeness, even though it is not considered by astronomers to be a very bright star. At night, when we look heavenward and see the countless specks of light placed there by a great and powerful God, they appear minute. That's, of course, due to their distance from us and from each other. Certainly, if we collected a small number of them, say a couple hundred, combined them, or concentrated their light into one location, they would dwarf both the light of our sun and their own individual light.

"Now I know some of you are asking, 'Is this church or science class?' Well, first of all, you know me well enough to know I'm neither a preacher nor a teacher, and that I'm quite uncomfortable up here in a speaking capacity. But the point I'm trying to make, being prompted and led this way by the Spirit of God, is this: We are light to the world, but it doesn't comprehend our individual lights. We must consolidate that light. We must combine our light with that of each other. We—that is, this congregation—must merge our light, our testimony, our confession, and our beliefs with those of other Christians across the nation to be effective in this age, in this wicked and perverse nation.

"Our individual efforts, as commendable and well intentioned as they have been, will not make the kind of statement to this nation that God now requires us to make. Our statement must be received, and we cannot fail to proclaim it. From this time forward, we hold the future of this country in our hands, and we must not fail. It's not just a time to regroup, reorganize our efforts, or to take one strengthened, anointed, corporate, and united stand. It's time to move out as proof of our conviction and evidence of our commitment. We are to put feet on our faith, as it were. If this country doesn't hear our message on a small scale, then let's give it to them on a grand scale. And if our nation doesn't hear us or refuses to hear us this time, then God help them.

"The essence of this word from God and is shared by our pastor, who has been hindered from giving it today, is to prepare your personal lives for divine direction. True people of God will hear the voice of God, not just as it comes from my mouth to your ears, but rather, from His Spirit to your spirit. You will know what the command of God is and where it will lead us. Our part for right now is to await His direction and timing and to pray for our pastor's release, so he can lead us on our pilgrimage."

After the service and just outside the church, a television reporter and cameraman approached Jeff, who stood shaking hands with the congregation as they exited the building.

"Excuse me, sir, I'm Vaughn Carlson of Channel 30 News. The cameraman is Harry Williams. I'm on assignment to follow this anti-abortion thing. Could you give me a few minutes of your time?"

"I will, but it's with this disclaimer right up front: anything I say to you from this moment on is my own opinion and nothing official for this church."

"My first question is this: based on what you said from the pulpit this morning, just where are all these people supposed to be going, and when?"

"That, I believe, hasn't been fully revealed yet."

"Do you have any idea who it is that will give you that information?"

"Of course, I do!"

"Well, could you tell me?"

"No! If you don't know the answer to that, then you're not supposed to know."

Harry moved around to the side, panning in on Jeff and Vaughn while capturing some of the milling congregation as well.

"Can I be blunt? I think you've got some kind of spiritual scheme or confrontational conspiracy going on here. These people are like blind followers. Is this church turning into a cult?"

"Jesus is still Lord here. He always has been. And as long as Jesus is Lord, there can be no cult. Our Gospel, which is the Lord's Gospel, hasn't changed. We still preach salvation by the blood of Christ, forgiveness, and eternal life with God in heaven. We also believe in the personal infilling of the Holy Ghost. Nothing's changed. The only thing that's going to change is the way we confront the social ills of this city and the nation."

"So you will be instigating some form of confrontation?"

"You said that. I didn't."

"Thank you for this interview. We're off the record now. Could you give me any statement, off the record?"

"No. I think it best if I don't."

"That's a wrap, Harry. Let's get the tape back to the studio and show the news director what the crackpot said."

Jeff bowed his head, closing his eyes, and started praying aloud, "Father forgive them for after better than two thousand years they still don't know what they're doing. They have been blinded, and only You can remove the blindness. Only You can restore vision. But we know You won't force Yourself upon them over their own free wills. Because of that, we stand ready and willing to respond to Your direction. Give us the victory, in Jesus's name."

The resounding "amen" from the milling members of the church echoed loudly down the street.

*****

Kevin Dillon and his fiancée, Sirinon Wangnuseeh, had just finished addressing their wedding invitations. The long arduous task completed, they slumped into the matching living room recliners in the home of Sirinon's parents. Just three weeks remained before their blessed day. Three weeks left to finish all the countless details and plans, checking and double-checking the list to ensure all was just right and on schedule. Kevin sighed as he tried to regain strength in his right hand and arm after addressing over two hundred of the three hundred invitations they had completed. Lifting his arms, he started signing his message to his deaf fiancée, mouthing the words slowly as he signed. "What if God calls us before the wedding? Will you still go with me?"

Sirinon smiled and nodded. The expression on her face was all the sign he needed from her. Then the smile changed to that of near ecstasy, and Kevin wondered the cause.

"What were you just thinking of, love, that made your smile grow so wide?"

She stood to her feet and walked across the room, sitting on Kevin's lap, wrapping her arms around his neck. Soon after the embrace ended, he had his answer as she communicated the thoughts that had raced from her mind to her heart and then displayed themselves on her beautiful Thai face.

"I thought about your question. The first thought was how great our God is to call me from my Buddhist religion, lead me to the Savior Jesus, bring you into my life—someone not afraid of my handicap or of sharing life with one so handicapped—and then include me in what will soon be a tremendous outpouring of His Spirit. How much more could I ask of Him, or expect of Him, or receive of Him? While I look forward to our day of marriage and the celebration we have planned, it does not matter if He says, 'Let's go somewhere else first,' for I am willing to follow Him at any cost. Should you not go, I will!"

They kissed. Then Kevin replied, his fingers and hands saying the words as his eyes released their load of joyous tears, "He will not leave us, nor will He forsake us. He is with us. And He will bless us here in three weeks or somewhere else when He directs. Maybe now I should get home. Tomorrow's another workday, and I'm getting tired. Say good night to your folks when they get in. Good night, my love."

*****

Satan was furious. He surveyed the situation from high above the planet. His clandestine operations across the country were starting to be attacked with a ferocity he hadn't anticipated. He knew all too well, from his past experiences, that these true Christians would, as always, call upon their God for help. He likewise knew that these true Christians would not idly sit by and take his subversive maneuvers, but never in his wildest dreams or schemes had he expected such a unified and frontal attack. Where had all these prayer warriors come from, he wondered to himself? Who was orchestrating such a coordinated effort?

His cohorts were proving themselves inadequate to the call of their master to resist the pursuing holy alliance. Why were these churches uniting, he further questioned, when all efforts to date to keep them feuding among themselves had been so successful? Breaches were appearing everywhere in the evil empire's walls the length and breadth of America. Satan, disgusted with the recent turn of events in New York, moved quickly to the next hot spot that was summoning his assistance. While on his way, he heard, off in the distance, the many horrid and desperate cries from demons all over the land. Demons, who through the ages had staunchly stood against any good and just cause, were now succumbing to the spiritual warfare of God's remnant church.

"Ahhh, shut up!" Satan barked back over his shoulder. "Hold on as best you can, you cowardly horde of incompetent rabble. I've a more pressing engagement that demands my attention. Take heart. We'll win yet! Okay, Atlanta, I'm coming."

CHAPTER 5

Atlanta

Larry Gillespie, a forty-five-year-old white male, stood at the intersection of Howe Street and Morgan Avenue. The large evening sun was about to drop beneath the blood-red western horizon. Fortunately, there was a breeze that helped cool down the record setting heat of the day. Although thunderstorms were predicted, none had formed. Larry had spent the day, as he had each day this week, at a business convention and was now on his way back to his hotel room. The crosswalk sign seemed to take forever to flash WALK; on the other side of the intersection was the bus stop that he needed.

While waiting, Larry noticed a very attractive black lady who appeared to be watching his every move. She was dressed to kill, and he figured in a split second she just had to be a movie star. More startling was the fact that she was now moving from her sidewalk bench toward him. She had to be, even without the high heels, about six feet and two inches tall, at least. The closer she got, the more intently he found himself observing her. Her beauty was strangely captivating to him, but he didn't know why. He quickly did a spiritual evaluation to make sure lust hadn't gotten a foot in the doorway of his mind. It wasn't lust. He then reasoned her sudden stronghold on him had to be due to his certainty she was an actress. After all, beauty like hers didn't normally walk the streets, he further reasoned within himself.

The crossing sign finally gave clearance to the five waiting people and one stray dog to cross the street. Larry started his trek with the mysterious and attractive lady right at his heels. All the commuters continued up the street except for Larry and the lady, who turned to the right, heading to the shelter of the bus stop, now nearly filled with waiting people. He sat down in one of the few remaining vacant spaces, set his briefcase beside him, and looked up at the bus schedule on the wall. As he did, his eyes met hers. Slowly, almost seductively, she sat down beside him.

"You're from out of town, right?" she softly spoke in a pleasing voice.

"Why yes," Larry answered, "but how did you know that?"

"There's a number of ways, but you just had *lonesome* written all over your face as you waited at the corner. Where you from?"

"Dallas. Originally from Pittsburgh, but my company moved me out there about three years ago. I really haven't been any one place very long, and it looks like they're preparing me for a move here to Atlanta. That's part of the reason why I'm here. I'm attending a conference at the Parkland-Grace Convention Complex, and I'm also supposed to determine if there's a need for a corporate division here in the north central Georgia area." He stopped his dialogue to apologize. "I'm sorry. I'm not being very gentlemanly, am I? My name is Larry Gillespie."

"I'm pleased to meet you, Larry," she replied, extending her hand. "My name is Roxanne. I'm not from here either. My hometown is Saint Louis, at least that's where I did most of my growing up. That's where my grandparents lived. They raised me until I was seventeen, then I left to come here. I've been here ever since. There's a bus coming. Where you headed?"

"To my hotel room. It's been nice talking to you, Roxanne. I guess you just naturally picked up that Southern hospitality since moving down here. Up north you wouldn't get the time of day from a stranger. Have a nice evening."

"Are you getting on this bus, Larry?"

"Yes. This is the one that takes me to the President McKinley Hotel."

"Well, how about that? This is the bus I'm taking too. Let's talk some more."

After finding an open seat, Larry allowed Roxanne to enter first and then he sat down.

THE STATE OF CHRISTIANITY

"Listen, Larry. I can imagine how it is in a strange town by yourself, away from home. Why don't we have dinner together? Then maybe we can find a nice place to relax and kick up our heels and enjoy life a little bit together. Does that sound okay to you?"

"I appreciate your offer, I guess, Roxanne. But the fact of the matter is, that wouldn't be appropriate for either one of us. I don't know about you, but I'm married, and having dinner with another woman, well…that just doesn't look very good, if you know what I mean."

"I sure do, Larry. But we're not strangers really. It seems like I've known you a long time, and anyway, who's going to know? We're a long way from Dallas. It's just dinner and small talk, maybe a drink or two."

"Thank you, but no thank you, Roxanne. I have plans for this evening anyway. It's Wednesday, and I plan on attending midweek services at a church two blocks over from the hotel. Do you attend church?"

"Excuse me? I think maybe I've misread you and the way you were looking at me at the corner back there, Larry. Forgive me. You really don't understand, do you?"

"Understand what?" Larry quickly asked.

"I've been trying to work a sale—you know, a trick. I can see now you're not that kind. My god, I remember ages back when I was that innocent and naive. I'd give anything to return to that innocence, but a girl on her own has got to earn a living, doesn't she?"

"You mean you…did you…I never would have guessed if you hadn't spelled it out. Maybe I am naive, but I wouldn't have guessed that's what you were doing. Roxanne, even though you might not be able to return to the innocence of your youth, you can return to God. Although I might not be able to have supper with you, you're welcome to come to church with me tonight. Or maybe you would like me to lead you to the Lord right now, right here. Would you like to do that?"

"Yes, I would like to do that, but I won't, or should I say can't, at least not now. Maybe this would be as good a place as any for a goodbye."

She stood and Larry let her out of the seat. "I'll pray for you tonight," he said.

"Please do that," she replied. "Who knows, it might just help."

"If you want it to, it will. There's no doubt about that."

When she arrived at the front of the bus, she turned, blew a kiss in his direction, and was gone. The bus pulled away from the curb in a haze of bluish-black diesel fumes.

*****

Although Larry had never set foot in the nondenominational church before, he felt at home right away. A spirit of welcome and friendliness greeted him at the front steps and ushered him in to his seat. Several people extended their hands in greetings, and even the pastor's wife sat down beside him for a few minutes of small talk prior to the start of the service.

Her lovely, peaceable, and charming personality became evident with each word she gracefully spoke. Larry figured she was probably in her late fifties yet carried all the radiance of someone twenty years younger. Her husband, Pastor Stanley Sharp, didn't have a gray hair on his head. Although he had some age lines across his forehead, he too looked much younger than what Larry presumed him to be.

There weren't any bulletins handed out by the ushers, so he didn't know what to expect as the order of service. As the sign out front said, "Prayer Group Meeting, 7:00 p.m. The Word at 8:00." That was the only order of service dictated by man. The Holy Ghost was apparently given free rein in this church. Larry liked that because it reminded him of his home church in Dallas.

He slowly and cautiously looked around the church, trying to do so without moving his head. He estimated the crowd to be close to two hundred, maybe two hundred fifty. All were warring in the spirit as though their life depended on it. How had they been trained so well to enter the throne room of God without so much as a word by the pastor, a deacon, or elder? Larry was amazed but quickly realized he was wasting valuable time gawking around the sanctuary. He stood to join in, making his contribution to the warring efforts of his newly found sisters and brothers in the Lord.

Gradually the intensity of the intercession decreased, people started sitting down, reverently waiting for those who were still in prayer to finish. Soon all were seated, and Pastor Sharp stepped down from the platform to be close to his faithful flock.

"You can turn your Bibles to 1 Peter 2:9 if you care to follow along. We'll only be using that one verse for our text tonight, but I think you'll find a lot of meat in there. I'd even venture a guess that you're going to be surprised as to the direction God provides in that one verse as well as confirmation to some of the things He has been telling us of late. Follow along as I read.

"'But you are a chosen generation, a royal priesthood, a holy nation. His own special people, that you may proclaim the praises of Him that called you out of darkness into His marvelous light.'[10] Another translation puts a portion of that verse in a much better perspective. Let me read a portion. 'Show forth the praises of him who hath called you out of darkness and into his marvelous light.'[11]

"Sisters and brothers, we are being called out of the darkness. Our four-year campaign to remedy the prostitution ring in this section of town has run into another snag. As you know, ever since the new convention center on Peachtree opened nearly five years ago, we've seen an increase in the number of ladies, and now men too, who have started doing business in our neighborhoods. We're at both a disadvantage and advantage by being located so close to the center. The advantage is that we have an opportunity to witness to the large number of visitors in the area. We can also invite to our services those who are in town for conventions or business and who might be looking for a house of God close to where they're staying. The disadvantage is that we see an increase in such things as drugs, muggings, drunkenness, and of course, the current epidemic—prostitution.

"I suppose by now you're asking yourself, 'Where's the connection with the scripture verse? Where's the calling out?' Those are two good questions, and they need to be answered. Like I said, we haven't made much headway in our warfare against prostitution. We don't want our younger children seeing this kind of lifestyle. Nor do we want our older children to have such easy access to those sinful and luring attractions. The city commission had agreed to place more police cruisers in the area at night but then backed down. They said they saw no increase in the crime rate for this area since the center opened when compared to the increase that's hit other areas of town. Our next request was to at least increase the night foot patrol. They again agreed but failed to produce a budget that would provide the increase in manpower needed to do that.

"Lastly, we petitioned the commission for stricter prostitution laws and more arrests, but this time they laughed at us. Monday night's meeting in commission chambers ended at roughly ten o'clock with three unfinished items on their agenda. The submission of the results of our second petition drive was next when they decided to table everything else for next week's meeting. We objected loudly. They yielded, quickly rejecting the petition due to, quote, 'the imposition of minority values on the majority of citizens not represented.' The whole thing took thirty-five seconds with a unanimous vote, complete with denial of rebuttal arguments.

"We're not getting anywhere with them. They're blinded. They will not listen to reason, nor even take into consideration the history of other declining areas of the city that have been plagued by this vice. They won't even call it sin. The best we could get out of them in the past seven months was to acknowledge it as a social ill.

"I know. You're still waiting for the connection with the scripture verse, aren't you? Well, here it is. You know all too well how God has been leading us from complacency to action. We've been found faithful and obedient to God in sounding the alarm and warning them of their sin. And seeing as how they've rejected the warning, God is ready to turn them over to their reprobate minds. But here's the good part. He has something new for us! Something that, if you look back at the past several weeks and months, you'll agree was the working of God. He has been directing us in our efforts and preparing us for a separation should our efforts fail.

"We are simultaneously preparing and being prepared for a separation from this darkness. We have warned them, but they have chosen to remain in the darkness. Once separated from them, they may then be able to see that *our* light missing from their landscape. They will hear our warning fading off into echoes. And maybe they will recognize the truths we've tried to make known—truths that become evident when illuminated by the light within US! A light that God shines not only on them but shines everywhere they run as they try to get away from it. There is no other reason, but this why you are here tonight. From among the nearly four hundred people who call this church home, you are the loyal, faithful remnant. You're here this evening to be marked in your spirit, readied in your life, and prepared in your heart to move as God directs. And make no mistake about it, God is directing us to physically move from this darkness into the light that He has for us to live in. Make your personal preparations! Make your spiritual preparations! And ready yourself for an adventure the likes of which you have never experienced before.

"Our journey in this life is about to expand to new dimensions and arrive at new horizons. I see some of the *wheat* separating from the chaff! I see the *grain*! I see many *kernels* fully ripened and ready for the harvest while helping others get ready! But this harvest I see is not the start or culmination of the end-time harvest, but rather only a preparatory harvest conducted by our God. He is about to harvest us, His chosen people, to a place of peace, a place of plenty, a place of unprecedented prosperity, and a place of health and happiness. I don't see this as a worldwide harvest. Not yet anyway. Not right now. I believe God is saying this and doing this specifically for America. This may be His final effort in calling her back to Himself and thus keep His blessing upon her. Are you willing to go?"

"Amen! Hallelujah!" the people shouted, jumping to their feet and raising their hands in adoration of their God and His greatness.

At the end of the service, Larry remained in his seat. Softly he began his prayer, "Father, I have no idea why You led me here to this church. This message tonight, though it moved me and caused me to think, was certainly a pastoral message for these people. Though I may try, I will be unable to turn my back on it. Although the service is over, leaving this place with the pastor's words still echoing in my mind and spirit is a near impossibility. And dare I even think of trying to get a night's sleep. Your message haunts me even now. It makes me wonder about their move, my move, and Your will.

"If my steps are ordered of the Lord, and I believe that they are, then You had me here for a reason. Am I to go too? Am I to take this message back to my church? Am I to move here to Atlanta to be a part of this body of believers? Lord, I seek Your face and guidance. I seek wisdom to understand that which You have shown me here tonight. In Jesus's name, I ask for Your help. Amen."

As his prayer ended, Larry looked up to see the face of Pastor Sharp, who was standing in the pew in front of him.

"Although you were praying softly, I couldn't help but hear. I'm not an eavesdropper, but my wife pointed you out to me as a visitor after the service, so I wanted to come over and welcome you. Is there anything specifically that I can do for you, my brother?"

"I really don't know, sir. You're right. I am a visitor here. My company has me here this week at the convention center. When I'm away from home, like tonight, I try to make midweek fellowship with other believers, no matter where that may be. Your church is close to the hotel where I'm staying.

"If you heard any of my prayer, then you know I'm a bit confused why the Lord led me here tonight. Your stirring message had to be a family message. Yet as I just told the Lord, you put some things down deep inside of me, and they won't turn me loose. And I'm not so sure they're supposed to. What's happening here, Pastor? Should I take your message for me or not?"

"You were here for a reason. God's reason, no doubt. You should certainly be on the lookout for His confirmation if the message might pertain to you, and if it does, what He wants you to do with it. I can tell you're not just a Sunday morning Christian. You have more to your faith than a soothed conscience and fire insurance. And I'm also as certain as I can be that you truly want the Lord's will in your life.

"Take what you've heard here tonight and write it down. Then write all that comes up in your spirit in response to this message. In this you will be serving two purposes: One, you will be making a record of tonight's word from God to meditate upon, checking it against the Bible for application in your own life. Secondly, you will have a starting point for further revelation as God provides. There may even be a third purpose, that being to consult with your pastor back home. See if he's been getting anything along this line. If you're attending a church like ours, a church with a similar spirit that longs to be pure and holy before Him, then your pastor will know what to do with what you show him. My spirit tells me this could be the confirmation he's been patiently waiting for."

"Thank you, Pastor. I'll do that. Thank you for taking some extra time with me this evening."

"You're quite welcome. Have a good evening and a safe trip back home. God bless you."

*****

Three days later, just barely off the plane by more than an hour, Larry sat patiently in his pastor's office, waiting for his pastor, the reverend Michael Baily, to hang up the phone.

"I'm sorry for the interruption, Larry. Mary, my secretary, will hold all further calls. Tell me, what's on your mind? Or should I say spirit?"

"It's definitely my spirit, Pastor. As I told you on the phone, my business took me to Atlanta this week. While I was there, I went to midweek services at a nearby church. As it turned out, it was a church very similar to ours, nearly the same size in fact. In my travels, I've noticed the diversity of people. And, of course, the same holds true for Christians. Although the churches I've visited are basically the same, there's usually only one major difference, that being their methods of praise and worship. It's even that way right here in Dallas. Look at the number of different congregations and doctrines. Well, at any rate, while in Atlanta, I went to a nearby church for Wednesday night worship. They started with a powerful season of prayer prior to the scheduled start of the service. Afterwards the pastor went into a message that was meant strictly for his flock. All the way through the sermon, while hanging on every word, I wondered what I was doing there. I wasn't part of that church. Why would God have me pick that church? What was in the message for me?

"When the service was over, I just couldn't make my legs work. I mean I could, but I didn't, opting to just sit there and go over in my mind what the pastor had just presented. It seems they are encountering some of the same satanic attacks that we are here. He related that although they have been faithful to keep the light of Jesus and His Gospel of salvation shining in their neighborhood, they have not been successful or victorious in the battle. Obviously, the battle he was referring to was in the physical world. He was adamantly certain of their victory in the realm of the spirit world. Am I making any sense to you, Pastor?"

"Yes, I believe I've followed you so far. I think I know where you're going, but please continue."

"Okay. I'm glad you're still with me because here's the important part. The thing that's been pressing on my mind and has caused me to come straight here after getting off the plane is this: The pastor of that church saw me sitting in the pew after the service. He came over, and we started talking about the message. He agreed it was a pastoral message from God for his congregation, but that he seemed fairly certain there was a connection for me. He seemed to think many churches across the nation were receiving similar instructions from the Holy Spirit during recent months. He told me to write down the gist of the message, meditate on it, and bring it to you for any local application here. I made a photocopy of my notes for you, as well as the results of further revelation to me during my times of prayer and meditation.

"Pastor, take a quick look. Do you see anything there that you might recognize as applicable to our church?"

Pastor Baily quickly began skimming the first page of notes. Soon his hand began to shake, and the power and glory of God filled the room. Larry could tell his pastor was experiencing a touch of God. He could feel God's presence like static electricity in the air. Larry watched anxiously as his pastor turned to the third page of notes. Tears were streaming like rivers down the reverend's cheeks and onto the paper.

"Larry, Do you know what you have here?"

"I do and I don't."

THE STATE OF CHRISTIANITY

"Here, let me show you my outline for Sunday morning's sermon!"

*****

"Where will all this end?" Satan asked. "Now my black angels are screaming in Dallas, Phoenix, Butte, Milwaukee, Marquette, both Portlands, and DC, and even down in little Williston, Florida. I need to go someplace quiet and think this through. Ah yes, Kansas—simple yet quiet Kansas. I'll go there and stir something up that will set the rest of this country on fire, and I do mean *my* kind of fire, not His. I'll start something there that will tarnish all He's been confidently building through the ages—His church. Hey, wait a minute! What's going on here?"

Looking befuddled, his anger growing into rage, Satan slowly toured the state of Kansas, pointing his gnarly finger at several points where prayers were streaming heavenward. "If my hellish imps can't keep things under control here, then I'll take charge of this battle myself. Take that, Topeka!"

CHAPTER 6

Salina, Kansas

"Tell me, Senator, why would you want to give up your powerful positions as state senator, chairman of the state finance committee, and assistant chairman of the minority party in the senate to run for governor?"

"It might appear on the surface that giving up all those positions, as well as potential positions further down the road, might cause weakness in achieving our party's platform objectives. It might also lead most political strategists to make one of two assumptions, perhaps even both. One would be that I wanted higher visibility in order to further my political career. The other assumption might be that I was a complete lunatic. I assure you, neither is the case. It's just time, in my estimation, that this state come under the leadership of strong, conservative, procitizen, anti-big-government guidance. Let's get as honest as we can. During the past twelve years, we've suffered greatly in this state under the hand of a spend-crazy mentality. Kansas needs a governor that will exercise fiscal restraint over himself and the legislature. He must slow down the government wheels enough to get a better picture of our long-range financial future, rather than plunging head long into that future with what I consider to be fiscal recklessness and haphazard abandon. And certainly, finances aren't the only area of my concern.

"I must admit to many disappointments during my tenure as a state senator. A major disappointment was the general lack of concern for all citizens some legislators have exhibited in passing special interest legislation, and the serious result it has had on many families in this state. I mean more than just the poor, middle class, or rich. I mean all families. If you look closely at the garbage that has come out of this state's government of late, you'll see how we've burdened the populace—young and old, rich and poor, educated and the deprived. The burdens have come in the form of tax increases beyond need and regulation beyond reason. I'll take some of the blame for not being vocal enough against those issues. And too, humanism has entrenched itself with its inability to strengthen sound family values. In fact, most of the legislation has eroded sound family values. Legislation that has been crammed down Kansans' throats like a pill somebody thought would be good for them."

"Senator, that's really the point of running for governor, isn't it? To stop or slow the passage of progressive contemporary legislation with a Harrison veto and wherever possible, to force the archaic, religious values to which you ascribe on the rest of the people of Kansas?"

"I really dislike that kind of questioning. Either way I answer you, I come off agreeing with one part or the other. You, and anyone else who cares to, can look at my voting record. It will reflect a conservative and cautious attitude on family-related issues and a prudent, vigilant fiscal restraint on all forms of spending. I look at every issue carefully to project possible outcomes that might impact our citizens negatively. That's not to say I am antipoor, nor is it to say I'm prorich. What it does show is consistency. It shows a consistency in all areas of government across the board. It shows a consistency that's been lacking elsewhere in our state government, except for a handful of stalwart legislators. And it demonstrates a consistency that's needed. The record also shows I've been thinking the issues and solutions through, not content to settle for superficial repairs. On the other side of the coin, the opposition's only consistency is the way they throw money at every problem in hopes of resolving it. The only two things that does is to hide the problem by keeping it well-greased and quiet while getting those who need real solutions to their problems addicted to the cash flow. And you know, ladies and gentlemen of the press, what that evolves into? Loss of hope! No future! For them or the state.

"I am not at all happy with what the past five years has brought forth in the line of laws and regulation, and yes, my moral convictions have a lot to do with that. The same thing holds true of those with the opposing views on the other side—their beliefs influence how they view the issues. Based on the regulatory and legislative moves of the recent past, Kansas might do well to move its capital from Topeka to Liberal. At least that way its name would more accurately reveal the general attitude lawmakers have toward most issues and the people who bring those issues before the legislature.

"My platform, as I enter this gubernatorial race is to prove the need to move toward good, sound, moral judgment, the kind lacking in our state leadership recently. I will provide that type of leadership, doing all I can to get this state back to the greatness it once enjoyed. A greatness we knew, experienced and counted on, that many Kansans have longed to return to."

"Come on now, Senator, we of the press are being hoodwinked. We can see antiabortion, anti-woman's-rights, minority repression, and a police state are the hidden main planks in that platform you just referred to. Don't you think you're about to commit political suicide if you toss your hat in the ring?"

"I'll tell you this with all the conviction within me, and God as my witness, if this is political suicide, and don't believe it is, then I willingly abandon self and deliberately and with full expectation of victory this fall, toss my hat in that ring. If nothing more, this campaign will bring the issues out and expose the error of our current direction. I, Richard F. Harrison, will be the next governor of the great state of Kansas. Ad astra per aspera!"

*****

In a basement several miles northwest of Topeka, the sound of shuffling cards and poker chips could be heard. Six men sat playing poker in a manner that clearly revealed it to be a cover for their gathering. They had each been paid a thousand dollars to merely attend the meeting and listen to their instructions. If they accepted the offer and joined in the conspiracy, they would be rewarded more than adequately for their services.

Jeff Richardson, a young-looking and even younger-sounding man of twenty-five, did the talking while the others listened.

"You don't know who I work for, and we'll keep it that way. I'll call him the Source. Are there any difficulties with that? If there are, you need to excuse yourself right now!"

He paused to check the response on each face. Now certain they were all in agreement to continue the briefing, no matter who the Source might be, he proceeded.

"The Source has told me that he's getting very uncomfortable with the initial rumblings from the Dick Harrison camp. At the present, Harrison doesn't show a lot of potential or pose much of a threat to the power block that's already in place. That's already been well established over the past ten years, and nothing short of a nuclear bomb, a direct hit at that, could change that growing block. That's why there's not going to be much mudslinging in this year's governor's race. No lampooning, no public debates, no out-in-the-open smear tactics. What will be used is just enough behind-the-scenes sabotage to keep them playing patch and repair. Just the same, the Source doesn't even want to hear of any successes in the Harrison campaign. He's in a place where he can sabotage Harrison's campaign, but he needs additional help from others. Call it a plan B, or backup material he can use at a moment's notice.

"Here's the point. He's confident that the fall election will go nearly one hundred percent his way. There might be one or two isolated defeats in the northwest part of the state, but certainly nothing that will erode what's already been built—more like a slight stutter step at the worst. But the one thing he doesn't want is for the gubernatorial race to look anything like a contest. If it does, that could change results all over the state. Right now, there's between a 35- to 40-point difference in favor of our puppet candidate that the Source is supporting. He wants nothing less than that in November. A landslide victory would be most advantageous because he could then use the term *mandate* to further his political and legislative causes.

"That's where you guys come in. The Source is certain that Harrison has a past that's not as squeaky-clean as he would like the public to think. There's got to be a closet out there somewhere with a Harrison skeleton in it. Your job is to find that skeleton or skeletons. As the saying goes, 'Don't leave any stone unturned.' We want him exposed. We would like a full-blown scandal but will settle for anything that discredits his character. Several wisely placed personality time bombs will have just as good an effect. With or without a skeleton, gentlemen, there's not much chance of his being elected this fall, but why not take his support base and party out along with him? Let's uncover some of his dirty laundry. We could even win that questionable northwest corner of the state if we take Harrison and his party out before he gets started! We don't want him gaining any traction. That's the job at hand.

"Oh, and by the way, and these are the Source's exact words, 'Don't come back empty-handed.' He wants a Harrison skeleton, even if you have to create one! Do you understand, gentlemen?"

The five men each nodded in agreement as Jeff again looked at each one of them. "Good! Are there any questions?"

"Just one," one of the men replied. "Are there any suggested areas of focus we should concentrate on?"

"Like I said, the Source doesn't want any stone left unturned, but if I were you, I'd start looking in the area of his religious beliefs. The Source seems to think he might be vulnerable there. Harrison claims to have gotten religion about ten years ago. That means even if he hasn't slipped up since then, and I doubt that, you ought to be able to dig up something that's still relevant. The one thing we don't want is for a Christian governor to start putting uppity, pious, goody-goody legislation before the house, and in the public's eye, every time we turn around. Besides that, there's too much of our progressive legislation in place that a Christian governor would try to expose or overturn if given half a chance. Harrison's just that type of guy. Those seem to be the main concerns of the Source. Dig, gentlemen! Dig until you find something! I'll be out there too, undercover, so if you see me, don't let on that you know me. Between the six of us, we've got to come up with something. Are there any more questions? Okay then, let's play some cards and make it look real."

*****

"I was very proud of you, dear, especially the way you handled those hostile reporters," Judy Harrison softly spoke and then placed a kiss on her husband's cheek. They were back in the van and on their way to Abilene for the next news conference. The drive gave Dick a chance to evaluate both the questions leveled at him in Salina as well as his answers. He was not only looking for better ways to answer the questions, but to determine if he had made any major gaffes in his replies. His campaign manager, as well as Judy, tried to assure him of his tactful and accurate responses.

"I still can't figure out why!" he stated out loud, but to no one in particular.

"Can't figure out what?" came his wife's return question.

"Why God placed it so clearly on my heart to run for governor. I've been a very effective senator. Five times last year alone, my vote made the difference on slowing down some humanistic legislation. I don't know that I'll have that kind of clout in the governor's mansion, at least not right away. Besides, without strong support in the house and if my vacated seat goes to the opposition, we will have a weaker position for our side all the way around."

"Chad Waldson could easily win your vacated senate seat, Senator," came the reply from Dick's campaign manager, Dwight Feld. "Don't concern yourself about that. We show some strong-looking candidates in over fifty contested house seats this fall. If we just got half of those, plus Chad and you in the mansion, which, by the way, will be nothing short of an act of God, we could start dismantling some of the junk that's gotten through in the past five to seven years."

"Dwight, those acts of God are called miracles, and we'll take any that He provides. If He wants me to be governor, I'm willing to be used by Him. We're not responsible for doing the miracles, not even starting them, just setting the stage by our obedience. If I'm governor next January, it'll be the result of His intervention in a situation that at the present looks as bleak and hopeless as it can be. But then, our God is able!"

*****

The sky over eastern Kansas grew dark, but no one could see the billowing black clouds that rolled in from nowhere in particular. After all, these were spiritual storm clouds, clouds of demons with business to attend to. To any humans who cared to take notice, the sun was shining brightly, and the sky was a transparent shade of blue; it seemed to tell all life that spring was on its way. Satan had summoned a large contingent of his evil accomplices together. This was a stormy conference for the express purpose of making assignments of individual mayhem. Quickly the orders were given. Quickly the demons were dispatched throughout the state. The instructions were precise, razor-sharp, and capable of exposing the heart of Satan's design—make the election of Richard Harrison an impossibility. And make the defeat a resounding blow to the conservative cause in every precinct, village, town, and city. Break those Christians' spirits and deprive them of the victory they seek from God. Dishearten all those followers of the Most High who started moving here. Given them pause in their plans. And do whatever is necessary to make them second-guess their recent decisions.

And as for me, I shall see what inroads have been made in that archaic mausoleum, that organizational relic of my Enemy. With a little luck, uh-huh, I'll destroy it! That's what I will do. Now let's be about our business!

CHAPTER 7

Locations throughout Kansas

Molly Fairbanks, administrative assistant to the deputy county clerk, hung up the phone looking puzzled and tired. She put a firm grip on her morning cup of coffee, hoping for a moment to enjoy the flavor and feel its caffeine kick. It was her first cup since arriving at the office, but she found it cold from being neglected so long on her desk. Although it was only nine forty-five in the morning, she had already been inundated with a stream of calls, causing her to feel as frazzled as at the end of eight full hours of work.

She turned to an associate in the office, Vance Tipton, and announced, "If I get one more voter registration phone call, I'll just scream. What's going on out there anyway?"

She had no sooner finished asking the question than the next call found its way to her phone.

"County Clerk's Office, Molly speaking. Can I help you?"

*****

Harvey Lendersen, a real estate agent in Wichita, hadn't seen this much business in the past five years combined. To be sure, he'd sold a good number of houses over the years but nothing like the volume of late. Since March of last year, he had sold twenty-three homes, five farms, and two small businesses. He was also busily involved in a shopping center under construction and the planning stages of a downtown mall. All the while he praised God, joyfully increasing his tithe to church. His move to south central Kansas had occurred only ten years earlier, when he became fed up with the big city problems that had invaded his Los Angeles neighborhood.

At that time, Harvey would have been happy if he sold two major pieces of real estate per year. Even as a beginner in the business, he just naturally assumed he would succeed in the LA market. Anyone, he reasoned, could sell enough to make a living, even without much effort.

But then youth gang violence became more prevalent. As a result, life in the suburban residential areas grew chaotic, and the effect on the real estate market was even worse. Harvey soon found himself fearing for his family's safety, as well as the security of their property. Whatever the cause of rising gang violence, be it peer pressure, drugs, demonic influence, or the prince of hell himself, Satan, Harvey felt compelled to move his family and start a new life.

After many months of prayer, he found himself asking God to show him where in Kansas to live. He even wondered how he had chosen Kansas in the first place other than by the direction of the Holy Spirit.

It had amazed him how things had turned out since completing the move. It wasn't so much that his reluctant wife, Betty, had come to love Kansas and especially the Wichita area. Nor was it the fact that his rebellious son, Karl, had come to know Jesus as Savior since arriving in Wichita. It wasn't even the fact that they had been blessed so richly in their finances. The amazing thing to him was that almost every house he sold was owned by nonbelievers while most of those buying the properties were. Over the past twenty-four to thirty-six months, Harvey and his wife, through the acquaintances in their work, had brought more than thirty families into their church, the Eastborough Christian Assembly.

Over in Russell, Kansas, a call-in telephone survey had been conducted by a nearby secular radio station. The results had revealed that not only were the vast majority of the respondents against abortion, but they were intending to vote in the fall for candidates who likewise took a stand against it. The survey responses, to the surprise of many west Kansas political strategists, indicated that no longer were the people in the listening area voting along party lines, but were now voting their conscience as well as their spiritual dictates. For the first time in recent years, voters were appearing truly interested in how the candidates stood on all the issues.

The week-long survey concluded that if the election were held right then, Richard Harrison, though winning locally, would be narrowly defeated by his opponent, who just weeks before led by about eighteen points in that section of the state. Not only did the questioning reveal an eroding lead for the opposition candidate in the area; it also revealed two other significant factors: One, voter registration was on an unprecedented increase among conservative voters. And two, of those who were registering to vote, nearly ninety percent were new people to the state of Kansas.

News of the survey results hit the ears of a skeptical journalism crew in Kansas City. One of the daily papers had reported the results in a small article, buried on page 8, near the bottom. A television station across the river in Missouri gave the survey results less than twenty seconds of airtime, mentioning it in closing at the end of their half-hour broadcast, and then only after taking five minutes to relate the Royals' activities during spring training. The facts may have been marginally interesting to the news media, or maybe even intentionally downplayed, but not so to everyone who watched the political fever of Kansas. They may have been less interesting to the mainstream section of eastern Kansas' population, but a certain unreported fact remained—someone was following closely, fuming at the news.

"Why haven't you found anything yet?" came the loud, forceful question from the Source. "It's been nearly a month! I would think by now we would have a shopping bag full of tidbits, any one of which would slow the Harrison move, but yet, I don't even see a smoking gun. Hell, I don't even see a single BB. Get me something on Harrison by next week or you're finished!"

"My people are out there working on it. Harrison's not an easy nut to crack. You'd be surprised how clean the guy really is," Richardson refuted, attempting to maintain his credibility.

"I'm not interested in being surprised! Mark my words! If I don't see a story on the front page by Wednesday, you're history,

Richardson! Do you understand? Remember, I said make something up if you must. A month ago, our candidate was thirty-five points ahead. Now that has slipped statewide to twenty-eight, thirty tops. If these are the results of working the problem, then who needs you? Now get out there and get busy!"

"Yes, sir!"

*****

At the parsonage of a church of just over four hundred members in Topeka, a saddened minister of the Gospel, Assistant Pastor Don Zigler, knelt alone in his living room, weeping before the Lord. The senior pastor was back home in Goodland, Kansas, with his sister, recuperating from a seriously debilitating heart attack suffered only weeks before.

How had things deteriorated so quickly? he wondered as he prayed. He was certain that he had followed the intended steps of his superior as well as the leading and promptings of the Holy Spirit. The pastor's last message prior to the attack was entitled "Get Ready to Receive Some Friends."

Only days before the pastor's illness, there had been biased news stories and slanted editorials pertaining to the large number of people moving into Kansas. The current edition carried an article that dealt specifically with the Topeka area over the past several months. The articles had been very derogatory in pointing out the rapid and uncontrolled increases in population. The increase of new families moving into Kansas had been unprecedented in Kansas' history. Such unexpected influxes in the state's population were expected to cause consumer shortages as well as subsequent higher prices, or so the trumped-up claims related. These were not Kansas' families, but rather "outsiders," as the inciting press labeled them. However, a caring Pastor Jim Tomlinson had lovingly told his congregation that the new families presented an excellent and increased opportunity to witness and lead them to the Lord. Or if they were already Christian, invite them to become part of their church family. At any rate, he never got to finish the message. Midway through the sermon, he took two, maybe three steps from behind the pulpit, looked up to heaven, and collapsed.

Now Reverend Zigler, just a few weeks later, was being summoned to the denomination headquarters to receive what he was sure would be, at the very least, a verbal reprimand. The summoning letter he received cited "questionable pulpit activities." He had merely continued the stricken pastor's intended thoughts. In fact, Don had taken them directly from the already prepared notes and outlines from the senior pastor's desk. Don had stated, in the ailing pastor's stead, that these new people could, when linked up with other Kansas believers, change the course of history for the state and eventually the nation. He was obviously making reference to the upcoming fall election. Certainly, Don reasoned to himself, if the pastor was going to say those things, then he felt they should still be said. And what's more, if these things couldn't be said by the pastor himself, then he'd say them for him.

Don stood from his prayer, packed his briefcase, and started the drive to Kansas City.

*****

"Welcome to this meeting, Don. Try to be at ease. I know our letter requesting your presence probably seemed quite terse, but I think you'll find this board to be less stern in person. We want to be fair and hear your side of the matter before us. Let me start by asking if you want to make any statement. Then I'll introduce the board to you."

The cold tone of voice told Don to be on guard when he spoke. "Sir, I think it well if I stick to just answering your questions. I assume you have some specifics you want to ask me."

"Yes, we do. First, though, let me introduce, on my left, Bishop Timothy Carnelli from Chicago, Reverend Robert S. Wattermann from Boston, to my right, Bishop William Connally from Dallas, and lastly, myself, Bishop Fred Hammond, from here in Kansas City. Now do you know why you're here?"

"I'm not certain, but I have an idea."

"Let me explain. We received a letter, signed by over twenty of your congregation, reporting you to be making political statements and endorsements from the pulpit since taking over for your senior pastor. Is that a truthful charge, Don?"

"Before I answer that, can you tell me if this investigation is going to be made public, or is it to be held in confidence?"

"I assure you, Don, as far as I'm concerned, what we say here is church business and goes no further than this room. Does that put you at ease enough to answer the question?"

"I believe so, sir. I've always believed we were unified believers at Calvary Congregational Temple. It looks like we are not. What I've tried to do since the pastor was attacked by the devil was to continue along the lines he had intended to preach."

"Excuse me, Don. How do you know that you were continuing along the same lines? Had you conferred with each other?"

"Certainly, we share together regularly, or at least we did before the heart attack. But because I had to step in so quickly for the pastor, I simply started following his sermon notes and outlines. He had about seven sermons at various stages of preparation, all intended for the same pre-election series. Fortunately for me, not only were some of them almost completed, but a couple of them were in final draft, numbered, and dated for delivery. I felt confident I was doing what I should. I still do."

"How so?"

"Because I've been earnestly seeking the Lord to not only show me what He had shown the pastor, but to prepare me to present it to the people with the same intensity, determination, and spirit Pastor Tomlinson would have, if he had been able."

"Don't you think, in retrospect that is, that God stopped Pastor Tomlinson from giving that sermon series, and now He's stopping you, considering this recent and apparent division and strife in your church as well as the events today before church hierarchy?"

"If you're asking me do I think God put that heart attack on the pastor, a resounding *no* is how I answer that question!"

"Now, Don, let's not get defensive. This is just a fact-finding hearing. No one's prosecuting you. Let's continue. Just what did you mean three weeks ago, when you said from the pulpit, and I quote, 'together we can change the course of history for Kansas'?"

"Well, sir, I can't speak for all areas of Kansas, but I can tell you what I've seen lately in the neighborhoods surrounding our church. We've had several unprecedented spurts of growth. Many of these new people are Christians who seem to be coming to Kansas from all over America seeking a new start. We've got new families from the Midwest, West Coast and the Pacific Northwest. And we are not alone. About fifteen churches in our district alone have experienced increases in church attendance, most triggered by these new families adding their names to the church rolls.

"Certainly, you know as the election year progresses, we are learning more and more about the candidates, their views of the state, and plans for its future. We're learning daily what they would like to see Kansas do during the next four to eight years. With an increasing number of Christian families, the pastor felt we should address the issue of voter registration and exercising the right to vote. I don't think I need to draw you a picture, gentlemen. If the Christian community can get unified for this fall's election, we could ensure certain campaign issues become reality, a reality that's in line with the Bible and our Christian beliefs. Does that answer your question?"

"Well, Don, I think it confirms the fact that you were speaking, or at least alluding to politics from the pulpit. You are fully aware of our church laws and internal doctrines, aren't you? You know we cannot tolerate that in our denomination. That's a direct and blatant violation. It demands action by this board acting on behalf of our statewide affiliation of churches."

"Sir, with all respect, if my pastor was going to say those things, and I'm convinced he was, then I'm just as convinced that those things were going to meet the need of our congregation. If I, as a minister, know the need of my flock and don't address it, that, for me, is a sin. God will hold me accountable. Your stance on that political thing borders on archaic, in my estimation, and certainly in view of today's problems facing America. The church is supposed to be the conscience of the nation to cause change in society. Maybe in this case, the conscience of the state. Things are not right in Kansas, and please excuse my grammar, but it ain't going to get any better if the church of Jesus Christ sits on its hands waiting for the rapture. We've defaulted long enough! I know you're not blind to what's going on in this nation. I hope we're in agreement when I say there are some things that we, as spiritual leaders, shouldn't tolerate any longer. God forgive us for tolerating them this long!"

"Do you understand the purpose, power, and latitude of this hearing and the panel?"

"Yes, sir, I believe I do."

"Then based upon your own testimony, we relieve you of your position at Calvary Congregational Temple, effective this Friday. Do you want to appeal?"

"Sir, I respectfully claim deferral rights in order to consult with the congregation before making that determination."

"Very well, but your appeal must be received in writing prior to the end of the day this Friday. You are dismissed."

*****

The midweek service started right on time. After the organist played a solo, the music minister led the people of Calvary Congregational Temple in two sacred hymns. Don stepped up to the pulpit somberly yet displaying a confidence in God and himself. It was almost as if he were saying, "As for me and my house, we will serve the Lord."[12]

"People, take a position sitting, standing or kneeling, where you can effectively go before the throne of God in prayer. This is decision night for you as a church. I know you well enough to know you always want to get with God before you make any decision. Let's do that together right now."

About twenty minutes later, the praying slowly subsided, and everyone returned to their seats. Don stood from his kneeling position and returned to the pulpit.

"I really don't know if I should be standing here at the pulpit or not, based on what headquarters said to me on Monday. What I must tell you is that this evening will be the determining factor as to whether I remain in this pulpit at all.

"As you know, on Monday, I was summoned by the governing board of this denomination on a charge of political activity from the pulpit. I was told that charge was based on a letter from some of you and confirmed by my testimony. Although it was only a preliminary hearing, the board found me guilty, for lack of a better word, and has taken action to remove me from my position here. You know what I have said as acting pastor. You know where our pastor was leading us long before his heart attack. You know that what I said, and what the pastor said, is what God wanted said, but you must now determine if you think I should appeal their decision. Obviously, not all of you are happy with me. The charges filed against me came from this congregation, although no one confronted me personally. Now it's up to you. Do we continue the course charted by our pastor under the guidance and direction of the Holy Spirit, or do we back off? Actually, the question is, should *you* continue the course, or should *you* back off?

"Yes, Brother Taylor, you have the floor."

"I can only speak for myself. I've heard nothing from you or our pastor that I find objectionable. The way our federal government is getting further and further from what the founding fathers had in mind when they first formed this nation makes it only too clear about one thing. No one in the government is going to give Christians anything. We've got to get things for ourselves. The Bible says God placed man on Earth and put him in charge of the garden. Somebody's going to pick up that authority and run the Earth with it. As I see it, it might as well be Christians. It's easy to see what happens if we don't. But what happens if we decide to keep you in the pulpit until our pastor returns?"

"That's a good question, Brother Taylor. If you want me to continue as interim pastor, all that's needed is a secret ballot tonight to confirm that. The results will be relayed to headquarters. They will, in turn, formulate an investigative committee to determine my effectiveness here and make a final recommendation to the governing board. And my part will be to officially appeal their decision to remove me.

"In the meantime, we keep on keeping on in Jesus. That may result in a split from the denomination. It could get that serious. But as the Holy Spirit leads me, so shall I lead you. We have work to do here. If you want me to be your pastor and lead you in that work, I need to know that right now! But I also need to hear from any of you, face-to-face, who have found fault with me in any way. Give me the benefit of at least addressing your concerns locally, rather than from headquarters. That's all I ask."

"Let's vote!" someone shouted from the pews.

"Okay. Ushers, would you pass out the paper and pencils? All you need to do is write 'Stay' or 'Go.' Seeing as how you asked the question, Brother Taylor, pick out four or five others to help you count the ballots right up here where you can be seen by this congregation. Ushers, one piece of paper per member, please."

*****

"Members, Brother Don, the ballots are 215 to 'Stay' and 28 to 'Go.' It looks like we have a new pastor."

"Thank you, people, for the vote of confidence. I hope you also realize this means you likewise have a new battle, that being with denomination headquarters. But we shouldn't let that stop us from the immediate call to arms. If we want change made in Kansas, let's roll up our spiritual sleeves and start praying in earnest. Let's also get involved individually in the political process and start making things happen for those candidates that share our views, beliefs, and hopes."

*****

Judy held her husband's hand as they stepped up to the microphone. They were in the friendly territory of their hometown, Concordia. A lot had happened in the past several weeks as they went from town to town. At first, only a couple of dozen people would turn out for a rally, most of them reporters. Now not only had the media coverage increased, but so had the supporters.

"We always feel so welcomed coming home to Concordia," Judy spoke softly into the mike. Her words bounced off the sandstone courthouse building at the opposite end of the park, echoed in the square, and then were drowned out by the cheering crowd of nearly a thousand. "We know we represent your values and your desires for this state, as we have known all along, because we've lived here and have shared those values with you as our neighbors. Now we've embarked on a campaign to ensure the government knows and responds to those values, protecting them for us and for our families. Friends and neighbors of Concordia, there's a whole lot of work left to do in making that a reality, not only in the campaign, not only in the election, and not only once in office, but in all the other contested senate and house seats. If the opposition, those responsible for getting this state in the sorry condition it is, are returned to office, it won't do any good to elect Richard Harrison governor. We need to do some sweeping, and I don't mean housework either. Friends and neighbors of Concordia, I present to you at this time, my husband and the next governor of the State of Kansas, Richard F. Harrison."

*****

The evening edition of the *Kansas City News* carried a not-so-kind story on the political activities of an assistant pastor in Topeka. The story drew a direct inference to the gubernatorial aspirations of one Richard F. Harrison.

*****

Bruised and weary demons were reporting back to Satan with regularity. Some of their news was good, but of late, a larger share of it had been bad. The consensus was that it was not a simple matter of whipping up on defenseless people. Oh, to be sure, there were those whose blindness and complacency were easy targets, but those Spirit-led Christians were quite a different matter. They were the cause of their bruises, along with the mighty angelic warriors from the throne of God. But what was compounding the problematic situation for Satan was the increasing number of people who simply weren't in Kansas just a few short weeks and months ago. "Where are they coming from?" asked one demon, looking like he'd been roughed up a bit.

"How dare you ask your evil master such a question?" Satan snarled. "You report to me in beaten disgrace and challenge my great battle plan with a question! Go find the answer to that question, and I will advance you in rank and position, and maybe even place you at my side. Otherwise, get out of my sight!"

Those pathetic human beings are sure right about one thing: good workers are hard to find.

Satan sat entranced in deep thought, rubbing his chin. "Yes indeed, the imp did have a valid question: where are they all coming from?"

CHAPTER 8

Topeka

"Now, congregation," Don started at the beginning of his first Sunday morning service as pastor, "I'm about to ask a question that we ask weekly and already know the answer to, so don't laugh at me for asking. Do we have any first-time visitors with us today?"

Nearly fifty hands went up across the sanctuary as the ushers scurried to distribute church welcome packages.

"We do welcome you in the name of our Lord and Savior Jesus Christ. He is Lord and King in this place and, more importantly, in our hearts and lives. If you've been here right from the start of today's service, you can tell we praise and worship Him accordingly. Our individual strength comes from the God of the universe, who inhabits our corporate praise.

"Let me do something just a bit different this morning. First, I apologize to the folks in the back on the folding chairs. We seem to be in the midst of a tremendous outpouring of the Spirit of God on the earth. It is more than apparent the recent growth of this congregation has caught us unprepared. We may find ourselves in need of a new and bigger building in the very near future—that is, of course, if Jesus should tarry much longer…I heard that, Holy Spirit. The Holy Spirit just told on someone. Somebody out there just said, 'Come quickly, Lord Jesus. Spare us another building project.'

"The thing I wanted to do a little differently this morning is to ask for a show of hands of people who are new to this church in the past six months. Go ahead, lift them high. Be proud of the fact that you're a part of God's moving. Oh my! Hasn't He been good? Let's honor Him and His graciousness by giving Him a praise offering.

"As those of you who are here for the first time can see, about a third of the congregation is new to this body of believers. Trust me when I say I'm not taking a census, but let's see the hands of those who are new to Kansas. Please don't be hesitant or skeptical because of what you may have read in the papers. You're among friends and family here.

"Praise be to God for His calling a nation together. He does indeed seem to be calling out a holy nation, a peculiar people, a people set apart, if I can paraphrase what His word states. In fact, the scripture text for the next several services will be in chapter 51 of Jeremiah. You can turn there while I say a few more things for the benefit of the new folks.

"Our senior pastor is presently in Western Kansas recuperating from a nearly fatal blow by Satan. The church has voted to not only keep me on in the midst of a denominational reprimand and ouster attempt, but has lovingly called me to serve as pastor until such time as he can return. We may be in for a rough time with church headquarters, but that doesn't deter us from going forward in God. We just want to be up front with those of you who are making home church decisions. We will continue to do the thing that's gotten us in trouble with headquarters. We expect to be a vocal pulpit as the fall election nears. Kansas, as well as other parts of the country, must make changes to remain under the umbrella and blessing of God. That's why we find ourselves contending with those in the denomination hierarchy. They believe we should remain politically silent. We do not. We won't tell anyone how to vote. That's simply not our intention, never has been by me or our senior pastor. What we do intend to do, though, is to reveal the stated platforms and beliefs of each candidate and how those platforms and beliefs stand up to the biblical truths we believe and hold on to dearly. Then we'll let the chips fall where they may, if I may borrow that saying from the world.

"At any rate, because so many of you are new to Kansas and this area and because you may be seeking a church home, we just wanted to let you know of our situation. We hope that by the time we have finished here today, you will know our faith dictates that we follow Jesus Christ, His Father, as well as the leading of the Holy Spirit. That, we hope, will persuade you to join this family. Let's pause now, this morning, to pray, asking for God's guidance and wisdom to enter us now and remain with us forever."

*****

The Source sat relaxed at his desk while dialing the number to a pay phone in Smith Center. Richardson was standing outside that phone booth and answered on the first ring.

"Right where you're supposed to be at the time you're supposed to be there. I'm impressed. I trust the itinerary, though quite demanding, is not impossible for you?"

"*Demanding* isn't the word for it. I've not been in so many places at one time in my life, but I like the challenge."

"Say, I read the story. That's much better, Richardson. How did you arrange for that to break so quickly?" the Source inquired, smiling and rubbing the short stubble on his chin as he scanned the article in the opened newspaper on his desk.

"Actually, I hate to say it, but I didn't have anything to do with that church story. We about exhausted the religious thing on Harrison and were about to give up. After all my research, I was convinced of one thing: Harrison really did have a genuine case of religion. I mean, he believes that stuff. I guess that it's part of everyone's search for immortality. The story broke on its own. We were turning our attention to his marriage, family, and finances."

"Are you sure? Have you checked with the guys you have working for you?"

"Yes. None of them would take any credit for that story. Maybe there's someone else out there with the same motives and intentions as ours. I really wish I could take the credit, but I can't."

"Well then, tell me, have you come up with anything in those other areas you mentioned?"

"We're still digging. One of my guys seems to think he's got a lead in one area, but it's not anything tangible yet. We'll keep working it."

"Fine, but in the meantime, why don't you do some rooting around on this church story. I'll bet there's something we can make out of this—that is, if you're creative. Do you get my drift?"

"Yes, sir!"

*****

Alice Ling, a data entry clerk and application processor at the Reno County headquarters of the Kansas Department of Motor Vehicles, needed the overtime but certainly hadn't expected anything the likes of the past month. Her part-time employment usually amounted to twenty hours per week, twenty-five tops. Starting a little over five weeks ago, applications for transfer of automobile titles from such states as California, Washington, South Dakota, Florida, and New Jersey had gone across her desk. Normally the small stack of such applications greeting her on any given day would be ten or less. Upon arriving today, though, she found, at last count, eighty-five. That amount would take every bit of her six-hour workday and then some.

"Alice, are you daydreaming?" asked her supervisor and deputy clerk Tommy Sarrenson.

"I'm sorry. I don't believe I was, but rather just wondering why all these people are coming to Reno County, and from such faraway places."

"You know the old saying: ours is not to reason why…"

"That's probably the best thing—not even try to figure it out. All I know is there are, as of yesterday morning's service, three new families at our church in just as many weeks. We don't see three new families in a year around here."

"Hey! Let's get to work. Don't start that religion stuff so early in the morning. I've warned you about preaching at me!"

"No, you got it all wrong, Tommy. I wasn't going to preach at you. I think I've told you about the Lord often enough to convict you of your need. I was just pointing out that there seems to be some growth going on here in Reno County that's not just a little out of the ordinary, more like a whole lot out of the ordinary. Don't you agree with that?"

"Let me see. I'll run a productivity program on the computer to see if there's an upward trend in ours as well as other areas."

Tommy's fingers flew at lightning speed across his computer keyboard as he first powered it up, typed in the special access code, and then typed in the commands.

"Land sakes alive! Lookie here! You're right Alice. Look, this is Reno's data right off the Topeka files. Voter registrations up…my gosh, it looks like we've doubled in just the past three months. And look at the vehicle registrations…just under a thousand in those same three months…and residence transactions…and mobile home titles…and…here you are Alice, title transfers. No wonder we've needed you to pull so much overtime lately."

Alice was now leaning over Tommy's shoulder watching the charts and statistics come up on the screen each time he keyed in a program command.

"Let's look at the state overall."

"Can you do that, Tommy?"

"Sure, it's easy. Just hope no one in Topeka is watching. Let's see. Yeah, here it comes…Wow! Do you see what's happening? It's off the top of the chart! The state coffers are probably swelling with all the fees collected over the past four to six months alone. My goodness! I don't believe this! Where are all these people coming from?"

"That was my question just a few minutes ago," Alice cautiously replied.

*****

Back in Topeka at the State Central Bureau of Statistics and Analysis, Jordan Crutchfield was monitoring the statewide computer system, occasionally taking a swig from his soft drink and a drag on his tenth cigarette of the morning. To him, the computer messages blipping across the screen were usually meaningless and not important—simple data retrieval commands or updates from offices throughout the state. For the most part, the computer handled them all. Jordan's primary job was to be available for specialized data requests or troubleshoot when the system's software failed. White collar all the way.

He had planned and designed his entire specialized college degree around the job he now held. Just a simple tip from the right people in the governor's staff let him know what the state was going to have as far as a centralized data processing and storage center. When the job came open for applicants, his was the only one that fit to the letter the requirements and rigid qualifications. Now, twenty-four years old, barely one-year-old ink on his diploma, he headed the department of over fifty other workers, many much older than he. Because of that accomplishment, he sat smugly proud of his use of political contacts while watching the monitor relaying incoming and outgoing messages.

Nearly choking on the last sip of soda, he spotted the string of messages to the small rural office of DMV in Reno County. With a few quick keystrokes, he froze the outgoing data to determine the validity of the request.

"That seems strange. What would Reno need all that information for? I wonder what's going on out there. Hey, Jack! Get me the number of the Reno County DMV office and the name of the head man out there! Something's strange here. My god, look at all that data. What are they interested in those figures for? Have you got it yet, Jack?"

"Yes. It's Tommy Sarrenson. The number's 316-555-8686. What you got there, boss?"

"I don't know yet, but I'm going to find out...Hello! This is Jordan Crutchfield in Topeka. Let me speak to Tommy Sarrenson."

"Sarrenson here. What can I do for you, Mr. Crutchfield?"

"You can start by telling me what you're doing down there with all that data you just requested."

"Oh, I think maybe I shouldn't have done that. I really didn't know you all would be able to tell we were making an inquiry."

"That was an awfully big inquiry. What's your employee number, Sarrenson?"

"Uh, let me see. I've got to read it off my card. Just a minute. 4556-0883."

"Okay, that checks. Now tell me what you're doing with all that information."

"Actually, I guess that was an unauthorized personal inquiry. You see, one of my workers here pointed out to me this morning the tremendous increase in the volume of her work. Normally we're hard pressed to fill her part-time twenty hours per week. But for the past month or better, she's been inundated with vehicle title transfers. I just wanted to get a picture of that from the main computer. It would be a tedious manual task at this office.

"Well, one thing led to another, and soon I discovered her increase was mirrored by the whole state. That piqued my curiosity even more, so I started looking at other areas. Areas like, well, you know, you apparently saw the data string flow."

"Yes, I sure did. I'll check that trend out at this end. As for you, why don't you stick to scraping cow chips off the bottom of your boots, cowboy! And don't make any more unauthorized inquiries! You got that?"

"I sure do, sir. I'm sorry."

*****

"Please, I beg you, listen to me!" the scared, quivering male voice spoke into the receiver of the pay phone. "Don't ask me any questions. And don't tell me I'm paranoid! I told you last week, and I'm telling you again. Someone's been snooping around! If they've traced it to me, they'll trace it to you. They seemed interested in how the *News* got that story on the Zigler-Harrison connection. Man, I don't want to get caught! If I do, you know it'll be my job. Hey! Quit laughing! This is serious! I'm scared some nosey-rosey might figure how the story leaked, and I'll be finished. Yes, I know you paid me, but that's just peanuts if I get fired or, worse, prosecuted. Well, the least you can do is let me know you'll take care of me if I do."

The phone booth door suddenly flew open, revealing two teenage thugs who proceeded to beat up the fifty-five-year-old recording secretary for the denomination headquarters.

*****

The crowd of cheering supporters in Mankato was down from expectations because of the rain. Still, the five hundred or so made a lot of noise as Senator Harrison reached the podium. He smiled, waved, and leaned over to kiss Judy and urged her to stand beside him. It was obvious the people came to see their candidate and weren't about to let him start his speech before cheering for several minutes. Soon they yielded to his raised arms and quieted to hear the planned speech.

"We're really making headway in this campaign! And people like you are the reason. Did you see the projections in the *Topeka News* yesterday?"

A loud cheer rose again from the wet crowd.

"I believe you did. It's only a twenty-point deficit now! But don't bask too long in that small victory. A loss in November is a loss, even if it's only by one vote. We may have cut the original lead in half, but there's a lot of Kansas yet to visit, a lot of Kansans I've yet to talk to. There's a lot of miles to trek, dotted with towns and communities just like Mankato, where the rural vote is needed to offset those big cities and densely populated areas. I know they don't represent you back there. I know their needs are different from yours, but they shouldn't have it all their way. You have needs, wants, and dreams for your towns too. Your tax dollars should come right back after they're counted. Why should you pay for the building, maintenance, and replacement of concrete roads in Kansas City and then have to drive on gravel, rut-filled dusty roads here? You shouldn't!

"But there's more to a governor going to bat for you than watching the taxes or paving roads. This is a different kind of lifestyle out here. This is an area of the state that wants a different kind of Kansas than what we've been getting of late. I know, because I've been fighting that trend tooth and nail yet with what I feel is only limited effect. I can't even use the words *limited success* because there's not been much success. You know what I'm alluding to. You want some of that humanistic legislation torn down. You want your Christian and moral values protected. And you want the murder of innocent unborn babies stopped—stopped yesterday! So do I!"

*****

"I don't know, Officer," the ambulance driver answered the inquiring Topeka city policeman. "Someone called 911, and we responded to the call. We don't have a name yet. He was just lying there, unconscious, and bleeding from the nose and mouth. I think there's more to his injuries than that, though. He didn't look good at all when we got him here to the hospital."

"Where did you pick him up?"

"Just outside a phone booth on State Place. Actually, State Place and Fifth Avenue. The receiver was dangling from the phone, so I suppose he was making a call at the time. I checked to see if anyone was still on the line, but there wasn't. That's about all I can tell you."

As the young ambulance attendant finished his comments, a doctor came out from one of the emergency treatment rooms, took off a surgical mask, and approached the uniformed policeman.

"Are you the officer making the report?" the doctor asked with a grimace on his face.

"Yes, the name's Officer Pratt."

"I'm Dr. Salyers. Well, sir, you've got a homicide now. He didn't make it."

"That's great! Even better than great! I can and will use that to my advantage. Just watch and see. Look how easily this species can be used, deceived, and manipulated. What spineless wonders they are." Satan placed his powerful hand around the neck of a small, trembling lower-echelon demon, pulling him close with a jerk and nearly decapitating the battle-weary creature as he did. "See how you can make things happen?"

The imp in Satan's hand nodded as best he could.

"Whisper a little idea here, cause a minor catastrophe there."

The imp tried nodding again but was unsuccessful.

"Use the power of suggestion to tempt some weakling into sin. Lower the boom on some unsuspecting soul when he's not looking. Voila! That's why I am who I say I am." Then pointing to the horde at his feet, he continued, "And you are what you are."

Satan raised the quaking demon high above his head for the others to see. His intentions were more than obvious. He was going to make an example of the imp to the rest of the horde who had been summoned for their shoddy work and many failures. They watched in horror as Satan's grip tightened around the demon's neck, making its head and eyes bulge to near bursting. Still, they were glad they weren't the one in Satan's fierce grasp.

Staring for a moment at the helpless demon while conveying some unspoken hellish curse, the king of hell changed his mind. With a quick flick of his wrist, he tossed the ruffled fiend to the side like a crumpled soiled tissue. Then with arrogance and pride, he broke the moment's silence. His harsh crass voice boomed out to any in his army who were still able to listen through their fear.

"Your inept attempts and mediocre efforts are still needed here, and I shall wield my authority and power in this place! And when I am finished, there will be no doubt as to whose creation this is."

Turning his mad gaze toward the earth, he continued, "And as for you, you simple-minded followers of the Most High God, contrary to what He placed in those so-called sacred scriptures you hold so dearly, you have yet to realize the ultimate victory is mine!"

Satan's eyes reddened with rage and contempt as he saw the steady stream of saints filing into church in Topeka. "Go ahead, pray! See what good it will do you!"

CHAPTER 9

Topeka

"Let's turn our attention to the Word of God, Jeremiah 51, starting at verse 1." When he was sure the flock was with him, Don started reading.

"'The Lord says, "I am bringing a destructive wind against Babylonia and its people. I will send foreigners to destroy Babylonia like a wind that blows straw away. When that day of destruction comes, they will attack from every side and leave the land bare. Don't give its soldiers time to shoot their arrows or to put on their armor. Do not spare the young men! Destroy the whole army! They will be wounded and die in the streets of their cities. I, the Lord God Almighty, have not abandoned Israel and Judah, even though they have sinned against me, the Holy One of Israel. Run away from Babylonia! Run for you lives! Do not be killed because of Babylonia's sin. I am now taking my revenge and punishing it as it deserves. Babylonia was like a gold cup in my hand, making the whole world drunk. The nations drank its wine and went out of their minds. Babylonia has suddenly fallen and is destroyed! Mourn over it! Get medicine for its wounds, and maybe it can be healed. Foreigners living there said 'We tried to help Babylonia, but it was too late. Let's leave now and go back home. God has punished Babylonia with all his might and has destroyed it completely.'"

"'The Lord says, "My people shout, 'The Lord has shown that we are in the right. Let's go and tell the people in Jerusalem what the Lord our God has done.'"'[13]

"Skip down to verse 13.

"'That country has many rivers and rich treasures, but its time is up, and its thread of life is cut.'[14]

"People, our pastor, while preparing this message, referenced that scripture text. I read it before going any further in my review of his notes. To be honest, it didn't reveal much to me at first. It may not have sounded too relevant to you either as you followed along. Then I just sat thinking about how the pastor had been leading us of late. I remember his final words before the heart attack. He said, 'And get ready to receive some friends.'

"Let me ask you a few questions. Who are the 'friends' we're supposed to be receiving? Do we normally have to get ready to receive friends? Now here's the final question: where are these 'friends' coming from?"

Almost as if he were waiting for someone to answer, Pastor Don looked around the congregation. Not content to stand in the pulpit, he walked down the seven steps to the main floor and down the center aisle.

"Don't be quick to answer if you're not sure. I know it seems as though I ask this question at every service, but let me see the hands of those brothers and sisters who are new to Kansas in the past six months. I've been asking it repeatedly for a reason, and today you're going to know the reason. Keep them raised high. Now would you mind standing to your feet."

As they stood, Pastor Don set his microphone down on a pew and started applauding the almost two hundred that were standing—young, old, black, white, yellow, and brown throughout the congregation. The rest of the members joined in the applause.

"Thank you, new friends and new members. You may be seated now.

"The scripture we just read deals with the corrupted, sinful, immoral, barbarous, pagan, and idolatrous nation of Babylon. The Jewish people were being prophesied to by Jeremiah. He had told them for forty years of their own sin and idolatry. Then at the direction of the Spirit of God, he turned his attention to prophesying the fall of the nations which surrounded Israel. This included Babylon,

THE STATE OF CHRISTIANITY

who would, under the prophecy Jeremiah was giving, take the city of Jerusalem and exile the people.

"The portion of Jeremiah we read of course dealt with the eventual freedom of the Jews from such future time of exile. All these things did indeed come to pass. Fortunately for Jeremiah, he got to see it and had the opportunity to say, 'I told you so.'

"That background brings us to the point of Jeremiah's prophecy and how it might apply to us. I won't take the time to reread the lengthy passage, but if you were to scan those verses, replacing *Babylonia* with *America*, you get, as it were, what could be a more modern, up-to-date prophecy. Also replace *Judah* and *Israel* with *the church of Jesus Christ*, and the prophecy gets not only clearer but quite a bit more personal.

"Now before you jump up and cry, 'Heresy,' I once again ask you to recall all the Christians who just moments ago stood, indicating their recent move to Kansas. Although we don't have the time right now to ask each one of them individually how it came to be that they are now residing in this state, you might be surprised to find they were led here by God's direction. Can I get a testimony of that by uplifted hands?

"Take a look around. If that's not a modern-day move of God, I simply don't know what one is. After all, if God did it once, does that mean He'll never do it again?"

Don paused in his sermon at that point not out of plan or purpose but because he came into a visual revelation—a further revelation of where he was and where he was to go with the sermon.

"Father God, I thank You for that which You are doing and have been doing in this nation. We are thankful that You have included not only the state of Kansas but this church in Your plan. We recognize, most Holy One, Your Spirit is moving and calling a people out from among the sin and corruption of this nation. We acknowledge You are preparing America for judgment. But, Father, there are still unsaved members of our families out there in the humanism, materialism, and every other kind of sordid ism. Although we do not know all that You have planned, we ask that Your plan allow us time, individually and corporately, to win our families and others to

You. Then, Lord, have mercy on our nation. So shine through us, Almighty God, that our nation might turn and be spared. I ask—no, *we* ask, in the name of Your Son, Jesus Christ. Amen.

"While it's still fresh in your ears and mind, let's take a closer look at three of those verses we read. First, look at verse 6. Can you see that someone is being told to run? Someone is being commanded to get out of where they were. It sounds imperative! Like danger is imminent. One could easily say the people being addressed in this scripture are being told to flee from the sin of the nation in which they are residing. There seems to be a warning that if they don't move quickly, they might be killed, along with the Babylonians who are continuously sinning in the sight of God.

"Now look at verse 8. On the surface, and especially after the warning given in verse 6, one might think this is a contradictory verse. It seems to make a point about Babylon somehow having a chance for healing if the medicine, or as the King James states, 'balm'[15] can be applied in time.

"Trust me when I say, the full picture hasn't yet been revealed to man. Based on what seems to be transpiring in our current time, doesn't God seem to be doing something with His remnant people, in order to serve as a warning or potential healing to America? Why else would He start gathering us together like this? Your answer to that could be right. He might be separating us prior to unleashing His judgment on the country. That might be the crux of the final verse we should look really close at.

"Verse 9 could imply that America, as did Babylon, won't even listen to our warning, and as such, will be destroyed.

"Can I get you to think on one more possibility? Might it be that God is separating us for signs and wonders that will indeed get the attention of an otherwise godless America? People, I don't have the answers. I can only see partially, but someday we will be able to see it all. We can, however, do this for sure right now—take our peace and our rest from the Lord. He will not abandon or forsake us. And the King of kings and Lord of lords keeps every one of us in the palm of His hand. Not one, only the betrayer, Judas, has He or

THE STATE OF CHRISTIANITY

will He lose. Take courage in the promise that our righteous steps are ordered of the Lord."

After lunch, Pastor Don sat quietly reading his Bible, preparing for the evening service. The phone in the next room rang.

"This is Tom Masters, staff writer for the *KC Sun*. Could I speak to Pastor Don Zigler please?"

"This is he. How can I help you, Tom?"

"I don't know if you've seen or know of the article about you and your denomination troubles that was in one of last week's issues. Were you aware of that story?"

"No, I wasn't. Do you have it there so you can read it to me?"

"I don't have it right in front of me, but the gist of it was that you were taking a political stand from the pulpit and had not only endorsed Senator Harrison for governor, but you supposedly took a pretty cheap shot at the other ticket. Can you comment on that?"

"Well, first of all, please understand if I'm just a bit gun-shy when it comes to talking to reporters. I don't know anything about endorsing either candidate, nor did I take any shots at either of them. I really don't know what you're talking about, and I certainly don't know where the writer of that story got his or her information. Do you?"

"Good move, Pastor Zigler. The best way to keep a reporter off guard is to ask the questions right back. I like your style. Listen, I just want to clear the air. Politics isn't my normal area of responsibility. We have a couple of writers out with a late case of the flu, so I'm on assignment in an area I really don't feel comfortable in. All I know is that you got in some kind of trouble with your denomination headquarters. What can you tell me about that?"

"That's really supposed to be confidential information."

"So you don't deny having been called in on the carpet, so to speak?"

"I think you ought to change the subject, or I'll have to terminate this call."

"Okay, Pastor. I have some notes here on one other area, if you don't mind. What can you tell me about a fellow by the name of Conrad Barton?"

"That name means nothing to me. Should it?"

"There you go again sir. It seems he was murdered over there in Topeka last Friday night. I believe he worked at the denomination headquarters in Kansas City as some kind of secretary or recorder or something I'm not exactly sure. Can you shed any light on that?"

"I think you're really asking the wrong man. I don't know any Mr. Barton or anything about a murder."

"Maybe this note I have here will help you. Mr. Barton was in on the proceedings concerning your last visit to Kansas City. Now do you remember him?"

"I was introduced to everyone on the board. I don't recall any of them being a 'mister.' They were all clergy, and it was all over so quickly."

"Well, I guess there's nothing in that story then. But thanks for confirming, in a roundabout way, that you were at church headquarters being grilled. I just wish I could find out the connection between the news story and the murder. It's probably so simple I just don't see it. Thanks for your time, Pastor. Goodbye."

"Goodbye."

*****

"I would like to answer your question, but I really don't know the church nor the preacher you mentioned," came the senator's response to the young newsman's question. "I try to attend services every weekend with my family in Concordia. Only if I'm not going home over the weekend do I attend services in Topeka. Even at that, I don't recall ever being in that church. What did you say the name of it was?"

"Calvary Congregational Temple, Senator. And its temporary pastor is a Reverend Don Zigler. He was quoted in the KC News that he endorsed you for governor."

"Well, I appreciate the endorsement if it's true, especially if it comes from a clergy. I hope it's based on my stand on the important moral issues and that we are in agreement with the Christian citizens of Kansas. But the fact remains, I don't know that pastor or that church directly."

"Well then, sir, if I might continue this line of questioning with a follow-up. This Reverend Don Zigler was recently in Kansas City, having been called into the denomination headquarters for being vocally political from the pulpit. Shortly after he returned to his church with an ultimatum, the recording secretary for the denomination, a fifty-five-year-old man by the name of Conrad Barton, was murdered. Does that name mean anything to you?"

"No, it does not. I might add, I see what you're trying to do with this line of questioning, and you might want to be extremely cautious in what you write in your news articles. You would do well to make absolutely certain you keep them factual and not filled with speculation. This news conference is supposed to be about me as a candidate, my ability to be governor, and my stand on the issues. I would appreciate it if you would keep your questioning along those lines."

Senator Harrison was visibly concerned by the arrogance and leading questions of the reporter. He so enjoyed the recent whistle-stopping in Central and Western Kansas, but the larger cities were a much more aggressively hostile environment.

"Well, Senator, I do have a job to do. The best way for me to get this side of the story finished is for you to tell the people of Kansas why your name, along with some other personal information, was found on the dead man's body."

"I don't know of any such thing. If it's true, why haven't the authorities contacted me? Check the police reports. I tell you I don't know that man, Conrad Barton. Case closed."

As Harrison fielded other questions from reporters, Tom Masters rechecked his story notes. He had the Harrison denial, but he sure had a lot of unanswered questions, including that personal stuff found on the body. Tom continued making notations, certain he was uncovering something big. Maybe too big for his mere three years' experience as a reporter, yet the compelling desire for answers wouldn't let him go.

What did the notepad with several pages of information on Barton's body have to do with the senator? Tom asked himself. *Why would both Reverend Zigler and Harrison deny knowing the man found holding both names? What was the connection?* Tom knew he had to have answers, but he hadn't been tactful enough in approaching either the senator or the pastor to get them. He really did feel out of place in the political arena.

Later that evening, Channel 22 opened their local newscast with the growing story. "Our lead story tonight on the five-thirty edition of *News Twenty-Two* is a slowly unwinding story about the gubernatorial candidate Richard Harrison. It's been determined that the name of Senator Harrison was found on the body of a murdered man in Topeka. Details are sketchy, but the dead man was apparently an obscure recorder employed by the denomination headquarters in Kansas City. Besides his wallet, reported to contain just under five thousand dollars and his driver's license, his only other possessions were a pen and notepad. The notepad, presently being analyzed by Topeka Police, is said to contain several pages of notations, many of which dealt with the senator. Police wouldn't give any more details than that.

"In other news this evening..."

"That's just great. Leave it to the press to blow things like this into near hysteria," Dwight Feld spoke while shaking his head. "We had the opposition on the run. We were making headway! Now this. We're clean, our candidate is clean, our campaign and its finances are clean. Now somebody's sabotaging our chances, and the piranha press is in a feeding frenzy for facts, substantiated or not, truthful or not. And you know they'll print anything."

"Dwight, don't be so concerned," the senator softly commented. "We're not going to get hurt by the press, we've got the ultimate Press Agent, and He'll make sure the truth is known. Judy and I have been expecting the onslaught to begin soon. Satan's not about to step aside in Kansas without firing off a few of his best shots. Really, I suppose we haven't seen anything yet. Besides that, though, look where we are now in the polls—only fifteen to twenty points behind and gaining fast!"

THE STATE OF CHRISTIANITY

"Come now, Senator—soon-to-be private citizen Harrison," Satan snarled. "You can squirm, can't you? Come on, give me a little squirm. I've had more powerful politicians than you dancing like puppets before me just for a little sex, some money, a false sense of importance. You're no match for me. I'm the great Lucifer. Can't you see I'm setting you up for a good long—no, make that permanent vacation from public life? Make me smile, Senator. Squirm just a little bit. We're talking murder here, Senator. Do you understand how that can spoil your frivolous political ambitions? Hey, Harrison, I said squirm! If you don't, you'll live just long enough to regret it, I promise!"

Satan had no sooner finished his threats on the senator than one of his errand boys came rushing in all out of breath like a marathoner after twenty-six miles.

"Boss…" Gasp. "You're not going to believe this." Gasp. "But listen to what's going on at Reverend Ziegler's house in Topeka." Gasp. "They're starting to compare notes, and they might just put some things together in the right order. Believe me, I've been trying to keep them all confused, and I've been doing a great job of it. But if they start talking to each other, I don't think I can keep things from unraveling."

"What!" Satan roared. "Another inept demon. You're dismissed! Back to the abyss with you! I'll check the good reverend out. Maybe he needs something to keep him quiet for a while. Maybe something like what his boss got, or better yet, maybe some more denomination problems. Maybe," he snarled, "something a little more permanent."

CHAPTER 10

Atwood, Kansas

"Yes, sir, we're following him night and day. He just hasn't made a slip yet," Richardson spoke humbly into the phone. "We watch every move he makes, but he's slick. Maybe we ought to cancel our contract. Even trying to make things up is difficult. The only one who's making any headway is the *News*. They got that thing with the Barton murder. Actually, they're doing a better job than we are."

"You listen to me!" the Source roared back at a near-deafening volume. "I determine when the contract gets canceled. I want you to call those inept jerks of yours off the job. Give them what they're due and send them home. You, however, you find out what the *News* is doing and where they're getting their goodies. Work with them if you must. At least they have something to start with. When we started this campaign, we were up forty points. As of yesterday, we're down to a fifteen-point lead. That's unacceptable!

"We have a golden opportunity with this Barton thing to finish Harrison off. Let's do it, Richardson! You hear me?"

"Yes, sir! Loud and clear!"

"And seeing as how I have to do your work for you, get with Jack Philips in Topeka. He works in the Stats and Analysis office. He'll give you something to work with along a different line in the meantime. And just in case I have to draw you a picture, ask him for the population figures for the past eight months to a year. You might get something to fabricate on Harrison from that. And I don't mean a whole lot of illegitimate kids either!"

"Yes, sir! I'll start right away."

THE STATE OF CHRISTIANITY

"Results this time, Richardson! Do you hear me? Results!"

"Ladies and gentlemen of Atwood, it gives me great pleasure to introduce to you, the next governor of the State of Kansas, Richard Harrison."

"Thank you, Mayor Johnson. One of my favorite towns in Kansas is Atwood. The atmosphere here reminds Judy and me of our hometown, Concordia. The only difference is we have a few more trees. But I didn't make this campaign stop in Atwood just to tickle your ears and talk about your hometown or mine. But rather, I've come to talk to you about *all* the hometowns in Kansas—the burgs, villages, towns, and cities. They're all in trouble. I know it, and you know it.

"We, the voters of the state, have to fess up to the fact that we've been duped in recent years by what started out as a small group of politicians jockeying for positions of power within state government. That group, once successfully in place, made further inroads into the inner workings of the bureaucracy while establishing their sphere of influence through political appointments—people throughout the bureaucracy owing allegiance to someone else or the objective, whatever that may ultimately be.

"With their machine in place and a candidate for governor who capitalized initially on a very charismatic personality, the will of the people got steamrolled into oblivion, or near oblivion. The legislation you've become so dominated by in recent years needs to be undone. The time will never be better. In fact, the situation grows worse by the day. The worn-out political war cry of the public to 'throw the bums out!' has more significance now than it ever has.

"While I appreciate more than you'll ever know, your support of my candidacy for governor, it is equally important that you elect a slate of congressmen and senators who will work together for change. Those who simply must be elected because they are of the same mind and spirit and will work with me to bring Kansas back. We not only have a unique opportunity for change, but nearly a life-or-death struggle to change, change that will restore the people of Kansas to their proper and rightful place—the ultimate authority and will of the state.

"The campaign literature given to you today defines the issues and the candidates that support those issues in the way you want them supported. Take those names to the ballot box and voting booths this fall. As for me. You can rest assured that I shall lead Kansas into the future the way you want it and the way God intended it. He's shown me His purpose, plan, and will for me. Follow what He tells you in your voting. Together, God, you, and I—we will make Kansas great once again. Thank you."

Meanwhile, back in Topeka

"I knew it was only a matter of time until someone official came to ask me questions. Frankly, I'm a bit surprised, Inspector, that it took so long. I've already had calls from several newspaper reporters."

"Well, Reverend, we don't knee-jerk react to things the way the press does. We need to know the facts and then proceed cautiously."

Don pointed to a chair in the living room in an attempt to get the homicide inspector, Fritz Anthony, to sit down.

"Let me ask you a few questions if I may."

"I'll bet they're the same questions that Masters fellow from the *News* asked me, but go ahead anyway."

"Can you tell me where you were the night of the Barton murder?"

"Certainly. I had gotten back early from church headquarters in Kansas City. I assume you know about my being summoned to Kansas City?"

"I do. Go ahead."

"I had just finished delivering my congregation's appeal of my dismissal to headquarters. It must have been just after lunch. Probably closer to one o'clock because I stopped just outside Kansas City for a burger at the first stop on the toll way."

"That would be at the Lawrence rest stop. Is that right?"

"Yes. I arrived back here about forty-five minutes later and spent the afternoon preparing for Sunday's two services."

"How about the evening hours, Reverend?"

"I usually turn in pretty early. I'm more of a morning person, if you know what I mean. I rise early for my personal prayer and Bible study time. That means by nine thirty at night, ten o'clock at the latest, I'm ready for bed."

"Can anybody verify your whereabouts?"

"Probably not. Other than the trip to Kansas City, it was a solitary day for me. We don't have a housekeeper, per se."

"What do you mean, 'we'?"

"The pastor and I. Usually we share the daily chores and housework but have a once-a-week cleaning company come in on Thursdays."

"So where's the pastor? Can he verify your whereabouts?"

"No, sir, he can't. He's in Goodland recuperating from a heart attack."

"So you're here all alone. Is that right?"

"At the current time, I'm afraid so."

"Did you know the murdered man, Conrad Barton?"

"No, I don't. He seems to be a mystery to just about everybody."

"That's right, Reverend. All that we have so far is what we've been able to put together from his personal effects, such as a notepad that had your name in it."

"Just my name?"

"Well, not exactly. It seems he had some other things in his possession linking you politically with Senator Harrison, something confirmed by your recent run-in with the denomination headquarters. Bishop Hammond told me all about you. He seemed really put out with you. How did you cross him?"

"Prior to that week, I'd never met him. I never knew much about him until that meeting. Before that, the bishop was just a name at the top of the list in church hierarchy. I've certainly got no beef with him. He was just doing what he had to do during the so-called hearing."

"Why do you say 'so-called'?"

"Because just about the time I thought he and the panel were going to start asking me some serious questions about my political connections, he ordered my dismissal from the church. He didn't even consult with the other board members. It was like a foregone conclusion, what they were going to do with me."

"That's strange. He seemed to imply in his answers to me that it was a very thorough investigation into your activities—extensive questioning, as he put it. He even held up a folder thick enough to qualify as a congressional report on ways to get more taxes passed. I just assumed from that, and his answers, they had been looking at your pastorate for months."

"They couldn't have. I wasn't even pastor then, at least not officially. Even now I'm only in the position temporarily."

"What were your so-called political connections and activities that got you into trouble with headquarters?"

"Well, it certainly isn't going to strike you as anything great. And it certainly doesn't qualify as sin. I'm still at a loss for why headquarters is so interested in me. I'm really just small potatoes.

"We were about to get into a candidate-by-candidate comparison of platforms and issues. We believe the Christian voter should not only know where the candidates stand on the issues but what the Bible says about those same issues, specifically on things like abortion, pornography, euthanasia, life sustaining systems, etc. We hadn't even gotten into that much of it when the call to Kansas City came."

"Tell me, do you know Senator Harrison personally?"

"No, sir. I like the man and his platform, but we've never met."

"You're absolutely certain about that?"

"Yes. Why do you ask?"

"One of the things in the notebook was an entry that mentioned a meeting between you and the senator. There was no date in the notation, but it was clearly written in the past tense, as if it had already occurred."

"I'm sorry, sir. There was never any such meeting."

"The bishop was adamantly certain you had. Were you ever in Concordia?"

"Yes, once. About ten months to a year ago. Why?"

"That's the senator's hometown. What was your business there?"

"I think someone's on awfully thin ice here. My trip to Concordia was to fill in at one of our churches there while their pastor was on vacation. We take turns doing those kinds of things. It was my turn. Headquarters just notifies us where the need is, and we go. My turn took me to...let me see if I can remember. I think it was Savior Congregational Temple."

Inspector Anthony paused to reflect on Don's words, looked at his notebook, then asked, "You say headquarters sent you there?"

"Yes. That's normal for them to follow that routine, although they usually schedule those actions through the mail several weeks in advance. This time they phoned me, but I assumed it was due to a last-minute change in someone's availability."

"It might not have been so routine. It might have been deliberate, Reverend. Tell me, did you know that the church you served in Concordia was the senator's home church?"

"No. Is it?"

"Yes, it is. I suppose you wouldn't know if he were there that Sunday?"

"He wasn't pointed out to me. I just had the two services and drove back to Topeka."

"Reverend, I think I smell a setup here. Maybe even worse."

"Worse?"

"Yes. A conspiracy. Your denomination hierarchy seems to be most interested in churches like yours who are, shall we say, more vocal than others. It might be part of a political conspiracy. Somebody's been following you and making notations that, when circumstantially laid end to end, hang you for murder and connect Harrison with a murdering preacher. Let's keep this under our hats for a while. Okay?"

"Sure, Inspector. Is there anything I should do?"

"No. Just wait for me to contact you again. Don't talk to anyone. And that includes the press and denomination headquarters. It looks like I've got what I came for, Reverend. Is there anything else you can add to help in my investigation?"

"There's one more thing that absolutely needs to be discussed here, but it's not related—that is, if you don't mind, Inspector."

"What's that, Reverend?"

"Do you know the Lord Jesus Christ as your personal Savior?"

"I appreciate you asking. I've known him since I was thirteen. And He's been right here next to me ever since. I put on His protection even before I strap on my .38. Thanks for asking. We're brothers!"

"State Department of Statistics," answered the receptionist.

"Yes, I need to speak to a Mr. Jack Philips. Is he in?"

"Who's calling please?"

"Jeff Richardson."

"And the nature of your call, Mr. Richardson?"

"I need some information for a story I'm working in my college journalism class."

The wait seemed long but was only a few seconds.

"Philips here. I believe you need some information. Is that correct?"

"It sure is. How do I get the state's population figures for the past twelve months?"

"Is this a routine freedom of information request, or is this for official departmental business?"

"I'm sorry, Mr. Philips. I don't think I know how to answer that question. I was told to call you for these statistics, that you would be my *source*."

"Oh! You should have told me this was for the Source. We've got your information all ready to be sent to you. And listen, are you using a pay phone? They can track location but not who was calling."

"Yes, I'm at a pay phone, like I was instructed."

"Where would you like the listings mailed, Mr. Richardson?"

"Send them to Box G-177, Kansas City, Kansas. The zip code is 66110. Have you got that?"

"Sure do. Need anything else?"

"I don't think so. I'll let you know if I do. Bye."

Richardson quickly inserted another coin in the pay phone slot for his next call.

"*Kansas City News*. News desk, can I help you?"

"Could you please connect me with Mr. Tom Masters? This is Jeff Richardson."

"Tom Masters here. What can I do for you, Mr. Richardson?"

"I know you're a busy man, but I've been working on a political point paper for my journalism course at college, and I can't seem to get it the way the professor wants it. My subject is Senator Harrison. I thought he would make a great topical character seeing as how he's already in a political office and also running for governor. Do you think you could help me by supplying me some information on him?"

"This is a highly irregular request. Why did you contact me instead of his press agent or campaign manager?"

"I was given your name by a college friend, and he said you were a good writer."

"I appreciate the kind words, but I'm not normally a political writer. I kind of just got it thrust on me recently. I'll try to help you if I can. What kind of point are you trying to make in your report?"

"I'm not really certain. I think, personally, all politicians are as crooked as a paper clip. I want to see if I can find anything in Harrison's character or personality makeup that would cast doubt as to his intentions or motives. How and where would I look for those kind of things?"

"I think you're biting off more than you can chew, especially as a rookie. You ought to start out simple, like a biographical sketch on the man. Harrison's dossier is an empty manila folder. He's so clean he squeaks like a new rubber duck in a freshly filled bathtub. You should have picked someone who's known to be shady, someone with some gray areas in their background."

"That's exactly why I picked Harrison. You can't believe he doesn't have some kind of skeleton hidden in a closet, do you, Mr. Masters?"

"What I think isn't that important. You should know a journalist must never let personal feelings or biases show up in their articles. If I were going to look for something on Harrison, it would have to be in the recent things you've already seen in the paper about his connection with the preacher in Topeka, the one who's being investigated for murder."

"Have you scooped anything on that area, Mr. Masters?"

"Well, look for anything that leads you to the dead man, Conrad Barton. If you check out Barton and can get a good idea of his involvement, you'll have a good chance of breaking a story on Harrison. Now listen, that's about all the time I can spare. If you find anything of significance, call me back. As one journalist to another, you owe me one."

"I'll do that, Mr. Masters."

Jeff hung up, made a short note to himself, and then looked disgustedly at the phone. "Rookie, huh? I'll show you! I'll beat you at your own game, Masters!"

"Ooooh, you really scare me, Richardson," Satan jeered, then added, "Just stick to the script I gave you. Always got to be an ad-libber, don't you? Why is it so easy to get such nonprofessionals. Most people do more to further my cause against God by accident than they realize. But just try to employ someone for a specific task and all of a sudden, they think they're the next Al Capone or the next Watergate reporter.

"What I need is a diversion, something to muddy up the waters and slow their inquisition down. Something that will pull them onto a dead-end path. Why yes," Satan said, with the corners of his mouth curling up to a devious and sinister grin. "Why hadn't I thought of that before? This'll slow them down like one of my hot tar pits in hell. Besides, Richardson is expendable. Nobody will even miss him!"

CHAPTER 11

Concordia, Kansas

"The senator will be out in a few minutes to hold a news conference. He will use this opportunity to try to dispel the stories that have been circulating about him in connection with the case in Topeka. While he, nor anyone else on the senator's campaign staff knows anything about the Barton story, it is apparent that someone is trying to sabotage his credibility and his reputation.

"Before Senator Harrison comes out of his home to speak for himself, I would like to caution you that should the questioning get what we consider to be out of line, we'll terminate it. I believe the senator is ready to come out now, and he will make a brief statement first before fielding your questions."

Dwight sidestepped from the microphone as the senator came out from his family home, walking the few steps from the front door to the prepositioned podium.

"Thank you, ladies and gentlemen of the press, for coming out so quickly this morning. As you know, over the past several weeks we have seen several fabricated news stories which have tried to connect me to the Conrad Barton murder in Topeka. These stories, by use of innuendo, hearsay, and speculation, have also tried to cast a shadow of secrecy and criminal activity not only on my gubernatorial campaign, but my character as well. I can only guess as to the intent of these stories and the motives behind the people writing them. Who knows what's fueling these stories? I call it reckless reporting when someone states as fact what they surmise to have transpired. No doubt my candidacy threatens someone or some group. Apparently, the best way, in their estimation, for eliminating that threat is to discredit my abilities or past record of performance. As for the drummed-up connection between myself and the minister police are investigating, that is completely unfounded.

"I have been informed by the chief of police in Topeka, as well as the state police, they have no evidence that conclusively indicates my involvement in any way with the incidents. All evidence to date is purely circumstantial at best.

"To try to dispel these vicious attacks against me and relieve the pressure my family is feeling because of it, I have authorized the investigating police to fully disclose any information that pertains to me or my suspected involvement—that is of course, substantiated information. I think you will find that information thus far used in these libelous news stories is solely fabrication, derived from a notebook found on Mr. Barton's body. A notebook which, at this point, has not been fully proven to be his in the first place. Nor have the notations been examined by a handwriting analyst to determine if Mr. Barton actually wrote them.

"Now what I'd like to do is answer any specific questions you may have pertaining to this situation. I would ask that you wait until my campaign manager, Mr. Dwight Feld, acknowledges you."

Dwight received a go-ahead nod from the senator and began with acknowledging Tom Masters of the *Kansas City News*.

"Senator, I know you just said that the notebook found on Mr. Barton's body has not been proven to be his. It could have been planted, for that matter, but is there any truth to the notation in it about you and the primary murder suspect, Reverend Don Zigler, being together at some time in the past?"

"As I understand the notation, it doesn't cite a specific date or time. To my knowledge, Reverend Zigler and I have never met."

"Sir, I understand that Reverend Zigler was at your church once, filling in for the pastor roughly a year ago. Is it possible that you met him at that time?"

"Well, that's certainly a new twist on a worn-out question. Had I been home at the time and had he filled in for my regular pastor on that particular Sunday, then it may very well be that we met, or at least shook hands after the service. I simply cannot confirm or deny such a scenario, but that would hardly constitute a 'meeting,' as past news stories seem to imply."

"Sid Painter of the American Press International. Did you know Mr. Barton worked at the headquarters of your own denomination in Kansas City?"

"Did I know? No! If you're looking to verify his employment, then you should probably ask the personnel office at denomination headquarters. I have no knowledge of who Mr. Barton worked for."

"If I may, sir, one more related question. Mr. Barton has been tentatively identified as a secretary/recorder for denominational headquarters and was so employed during the dismissal hearing of Reverend Zigler. The reverend denies this fact or at least any knowledge of it, yet another notation in the notebook read something to the effect 'Rev. Z to be dismissed for supporting R. H. B. H. + inside + info = dead end.' Would you know how to interpret that notation?"

"No, I would not."

Dwight recognized several other reporters who took their turn hammering the senator on their various speculative questions. Soon it got out of hand, and the news conference was terminated.

*****

Fritz Anthony stood near the front window of the cafe across the street from the north side branch of the Kansas City post office. The building had been staked out ever since the package from the Bureau of Stats and Analysis had arrived earlier in the day. Fritz had patiently waited for the first four hours, yielding to a relief man in order to have lunch and to check in at police headquarters. He was now back, waiting and diligently watching the front of the building. Inside the post office, behind the wall of boxes, stood a uniformed Kansas City policeman with a walkie-talkie, ready to communicate to Fritz when the box was opened and its contents retrieved. Fritz looked at his watch. It was nearly 9:30 p.m., and he decided to have one more cup of coffee and then head back to his motel room.

"Fritz, the window's open!" the officer in the post office reported over the radio in a whispered voice. "The parcel's out now and heading for the door," were the next words to come across Fritz's receiver. The quick announcement caught him by surprise, nearly causing him to spill his coffee. Setting the cup back in the saucer, he hurriedly made his way to the door, out into the damp night air, and across the empty street.

He approached Richardson cautiously, retrieved his badge, and made ready to identify himself.

"Mr. Richardson. I'm Inspector Anthony, Topeka Police. Can I ask you a few questions about the package you just got from your post office box?"

"Did you say 'Topeka'? A little bit out of your district, aren't you?"

"Yes, but I think you'll recognize the uniform of the Kansas City police officer behind you. Now can I ask you some questions?"

"For the time being."

"You can start by telling me what's in the package."

"Just computerized statistics."

"What do you need them for?"

"A college journalism class project."

"Do you know anyone by the name Conrad Barton?"

"No."

"How about a Reverend Zigler?"

"Where is all this leading? Do I look like some religious freak? I don't know any Reverend...what did you say?"

"Zigler."

"No."

"How about Senator Harrison?"

"Sure, I know of him, but nothing more than that."

"Do you want to change that answer?"

"No. Now if you're done asking questions, can I leave?"

"I'm not done asking so stay put. I have two other things I would like to know. First, if you don't know anyone by the name of Barton or Zigler, why did you call a Tom Masters at the *News* for information about Barton's murder, Zigler's involvement, and Harrison's connection?"

"I didn't ask about those things. Masters volunteered that stuff."

"You just made a mistake, mister. Officer, book him on suspicion."

"Hey! What are you doing? Suspicion of what?"

"Murder good enough for you, Richardson?"

"Hey, you got it all wrong! I'm telling you, I'm writing a news article for a college class. Masters told me to look into those areas. I didn't murder anyone! You're nuts! Hey, you're hurting my wrists!"

"We serve an all-knowing God, and because of that, we can trust Him to do whatever's necessary to accomplish His purpose." Pastor Don had made a smooth transition from receiving the midweek's tithes and offerings, through a few minor announcements, then into the opening sentence of his sermon.

"Our sermon line will continue, as it has for the past several weeks, to deal with how God is preparing His church—that's us—to accomplish His plan, a plan that reveals not only a separating of His people, but His preparing to judge the forces of evil that now permeate this once great nation. A nation that seems bent on being guided by satanic influence or, at the very least, to follow the dictates of the flesh.

"For right now, though, we need to consult His holy Word for our guidance. There are two specific areas I would like to look at closely. But before we get into the study for this evening, could the ushers please put up several more folding chairs across the back and down the center aisle to accommodate any late arrivals. Then let's leave them that way for future services rather than making noises setting them up as needed. The distraction isn't so bothersome to me as it is to those who are trying diligently to receive the Word of God. Thank you.

"Turn first to Matthew 10:23 and follow as I read. 'But when they persecute you in this city, flee ye into another: for verily I say unto you, Ye shall not have gone over the cities of Israel, till the Son of man be come.'[16]

"Shall we pray? Our Father and our God, we thank You for Your Word. It is indeed a lamp unto our feet and a light unto our path. One of the amazing things about Your Word, oh Lord, is the timelessness of it. Though inspired and written centuries, even millennia ago, it falters not as time progresses. It validates itself time and time again. It talks to us, we who are Your Son's church, a people You have gathered unto Yourself. Yet it instructs us individually. It has done so to those who have recently followed Your instruction, leaving all and coming here to this state, this city, and this church. And too, Your Word has spoken to those of us not asked to move but rather to stay and to receive those whom You have moved.

"The words we just read were originally addressed to the first members of Your church, Lord Jesus. You told them up front that persecution would be a part of following You. You didn't hide anything from them when You informed those faithful first few of the eventual need to flee, not as scared rabbits or hunted wild dogs, but rather to take their message of hope and the blessing of God to a people who would receive it rather than wasting it on those who wouldn't accept it. They were, in another scripture, told to shake the dust from their feet of the towns that would not receive the visitation of truth.

"How like You it is that You would give the saints of old guidance, see to it that it was recorded, and make that same truth relevant to us who seek it today. We trust in Your Word and ask You to reveal more of it to our spirits as we ask and pray in the holy name of Jesus. Amen."

*****

"I'm not going to say anything else until I have an attorney appointed. I know my rights!"

"Okay, Richardson, we'll see to it that you get representation. Officer, put him back in the cell."

Fritz sat back down in the chair, scratching his head.

"I just don't understand his involvement," he said, looking directly into the face of Richardson's arresting officer, Trent Varney.

THE STATE OF CHRISTIANITY

"He admits making the call to the Bureau of Stats and Analysis, but he sticks to this journalism story. I'll be glad when we can talk to his college professor. He didn't even seem concerned about the fact that we were following him. That would scare most characters on their first arrest into spilling their guts, especially when facing a possible murder charge. I'm convinced he's just an entry-level worker in someone's scheme, a scheme that's beginning to make a murderer out of an otherwise innocent preacher.

"What do you make of these statistics?" Fritz asked Officer Varney while pointing to the pile of numerical spreadsheets and statistical summaries.

"I don't really know. They seem to fit what he said about his college writing project. I'd be hard-pressed to believe the state's population has increased as much as these statistics show, but you can't argue with cold, hard facts. Look here. Here's the Wyandotte County figures. That's the county you're in right now. The population's up in the past twelve months by over twenty percent. That's a tremendous increase in anybody's books."

Fritz turned the statistics around to get a better look at what Officer Varney was showing him. "But I don't understand what that's got to do with Richardson's interest in Harrison. Masters said that Richardson told him he was interested in proving that Harrison had a skeleton someplace. Does he think that if he digs deep and long enough, he can prove his point and thus get a good grade on his writing assignment, or is there something else to all of this? I'm just not so certain that school's his only motive. Besides that, what do these figures show that would interest him or help him prove his objective? There's got to be more here than cold, hard facts."

"Well," Varney offered, "he said he was employed as a part-time investigator. Maybe that's just his instinct or style—you know, looking under every rock."

"That's a possibility. It could be just as he says. We may very well be looking at all the wrong things, making it look more complex than it is. I just don't know! I feel uneasy about this."

Almost in an effort to release his increasing frustration, Fritz fanned through several more pages of the statistics as if riffling through a magazine. He allowed the pages to fall open wherever his fanning stopped. Then he paused, about to leave for his hotel room, all his muscles poised to lift him from the hard wooden chair, when the open page grabbed his curiosity, jerking his attention to the chart before him.

"Maybe this is it. Maybe this is...Look, Varney! See what this chart reflects? Not only has the population exploded here and across the state, look what else has exploded. Why didn't I think of that? It just naturally follows, doesn't it? With each elevation in population figures comes a corresponding increase in voter registration. Future voters who, being new to the state's politics, need to be kept away from the Harrison fold. How was he intending to do that—or was he? Maybe he's much smarter than I've given him credit for.

"As soon as an attorney gets appointed, I want to talk to Richardson again. If I get nothing else, I want to know who's behind his activity. I'm going to go to my motel room, shower, and shave. I'll be back shortly."

The congregation sat attentively, hanging on every word as Pastor Don continued his message. "Let's turn now to the book of Revelation. Specifically, chapters 18 and 19. I'm going to read them very slowly, allowing the Spirit of God to cause the words to settle deep within your spirit. Please pay close attention, weighing what you hear against all that has been said of late, all that's been happening in this nation, and especially here in Kansas."

*****

Officer Varney introduced Mr. James Walters, the state-appointed attorney for Jeff Richardson, to Inspector Anthony.

"Do you feel ready to start the questioning?" Fritz asked of Walters.

"Yes. I've had consultation with my client, and we're ready to begin."

"Good. I think everyone here wants to get this matter cleared up, so let me start by asking some basic background questions. First, what college are you attending, Mr. Richardson?"

"Kansas City State Community College."
"How many courses are you taking?"
"Just one—a journalism class."
"What do you do for a living?"
"I work occasionally for a private business doing investigating."
"Can you name this business?"
"I'd rather not."
"Any particular reason why you wouldn't?"

Quickly Mr. Walters interjected, "That's not relevant to what we're doing here. I've advised my client not to answer any questions that are not relevant to the arrest. If he's in doubt, I'll give him a nod if he should answer, otherwise, no answer."

"Okay. Let's move on then to the journalism class. Who is your professor in that class?"

"Dr. Rachel Hemstead."
"That's a lady professor?"
"Yes."
"What is the assignment you're presently working on for her class?"

"An investigative story on a political figure of our choice."
"Who did you select?"
"Senator Richard Harrison."
"Any particular reason for selecting him?"
"Yes, he's both in a political office and running for one as well. That made him interesting to me."
"Any other reason for selecting him?"
"None."

Fritz got up from his chair and walked over to a table on the other side of the room, placing his hand upon the pile of papers containing the population stats sent to Richardson. Turning back toward Jeff, he continued his questioning.

"Earlier tonight you said that a reporter for the *News* had advised you to look at Harrison from the perspective of his connection with a Reverend Zigler and a Conrad Barton. What did you find out about that connection?"

"I was checking out Harrison's character to see if he was really as squeaky-clean as he looks. Call it grabbing at straws, but I needed to get a good grade on this paper. My grades have been down a little this marking period."

"Forgive me if I don't buy that. What were you going to do with those statistics you received earlier tonight?"

"I was, like I said, grabbing at straws. Someone told me to look at how the population was growing in areas where Harrison was weak. That didn't make any sense to me at all, but I needed to know if there was some hanky-panky in the voter demographics."

Fritz moved close in to face Jeff, attempting to read the story in his eyes. "I talked to Dr. Hemstead on the phone about twenty minutes ago. She said her grade book reflected your grades were very good. In fact, her exact words were, 'top 3 in the class,' and what's more, the college admissions office said this is your first class. That doesn't support your claim to falling grades."

"I don't see what you're driving at," Richardson's attorney firmly stated. You have my client booked on suspicion of murder, let's get to the point. Otherwise, release him."

"Okay, we'll fill in the fine cracks later. So you knew of the Zigler-Barton-Harrison connection?"

"Only at the direction of Tom Masters at the *News*."

"What did he tell you?"

"To look into the murder thing. He implied that Harrison was being supported or endorsed by Zigler and Zigler killed that Barton fellow. He seemed to think there was a story there. I haven't found one yet, or at least I haven't had time to find one yet. And I'll bet Masters doesn't find one either. It all looks superficial to me. I guess others in the press are having a field day with the innuendoes and 'reliable sources,' but there's nothing there I could use for the journalism assignment, at least not to me. Dr. Hemstead wouldn't stand for use of those kinds of tactics in her assignments. She'd give me an F for sure.

"Tell me, then, how did you get these statistics from the State Bureau of Stats and Analysis?"

"I just phoned the office. I was given a name, Jack Philips, as a point of contact. I called him, and he sent them out to me. That's all there is to that."

"Did you fill in a request for information form?"

"No. I wasn't told I had to."

"Who gave you Philips's name?"

"I don't know his name."

"Come again, Richardson. Who told you to call Philips?"

"I don't know who. It was a tip from a stranger on the phone who called me. I didn't call him."

"Excuse me, but I'm having trouble with some of your answers. Let me tell you that your name came up several times during our investigation. Though not a legitimate member of the press, you have been following Harrison with a press pass for nearly three months. How did you get that pass?"

Richardson and Walters conferred for a moment.

"My client cannot answer that due to self-incrimination."

"Let me also tell you that we have a copy of phone company records for your phone. There's a pretty good history of long-distance calls you have been making and billing to your home phone. That history indicates, when compared to Senator Harrison's recent campaign itinerary, that you have indeed been following the senator and have been talking to a lot of people whose names have come up in our investigation. One number in particular, 913-985-6564, shows up quite frequently. Do you know whose number that is?"

"Not right off the top of my head."

"Well, let me refresh your memory. It's a pay phone here in Kansas City. Does that help you any?"

"No!"

Walters stood, looking annoyed, then proceeded to talk while pointing his finger into Fritz's chest. "I think I want this questioning to stop. If you don't have some hard evidence for my client to respond to about the Barton murder, then sign his release."

"We've got more specific things to discuss, but now is not the time. We can hold him for another, let's see, nineteen hours. And hold him we will."

*****

"Dear people of God," Pastor Don pressed forward into the meatier part of his lengthy sermon. "We cannot be like ostriches and bury our heads in the sand. We cannot hope for things to get better. We must make them better. Remember that God placed man in charge in the earth. It's our God-given responsibility to 'tend the garden.' Mankind has strayed from the instruction book, the operating manual if you will, the Bible, thus allowing the prince of the air to enter what is supposed to be our domain, not his. His occupation is to steal, kill, and destroy, and he's doing a good and thorough job of it.

"We, the body of Christ, are getting positioned to show what the prophecy of Revelation 18 and 19 could—I didn't say *was*, I said *could* be talking about. Look at verse 2 in chapter 18. Babylon is described as a 'habitation of devils and holds every foul spirit.'[17] Couldn't we say the same thing of America?

"Verse 3 says, 'All nations have drunk of the wine of wrath of her fornication.' Hasn't the decadence found in America spread to other nations by our deliberate influence? Verse 3 also says, 'Merchants grew rich through the abundance of her delicacies.'[18] Hasn't our abundance been marveled at and copied throughout many other nations of the world?

"Verse 4 warns God's people to 'come out of her,' her being Babylon, and 'be not partakers in the sins of the land.'[19] God doesn't want His people to suffer the plagues that are to be experienced. I imagine some of our newly arrived brothers and sisters have heard words along this same line prior to heading for Kansas. Can the rest of you see how God has directed these lovely people here to join us in His future purpose, whatever that may be? The urgency of the directive leads me to believe we're going to see that purpose soon.

THE STATE OF CHRISTIANITY

"We've discussed recently the sins of this nation, sins so numerous that they, more often than not, seem to be the norms of life, but they do not go unnoticed by God. Look and read verse 5. Enough said?

"Verses 6 through 10 tell of destruction, destruction for Babylon, but could it not be for America as well? Remember how the recorded events surrounding the battle of Armageddon show Russia, Europe and Israel but don't even mention a western-world country? There's just no mention of an eagle from the west, only a bear from the north. Could it be that by that time, sometime in the future, there is no eagle from the west? All I'm asking you to do is think about it. This may not be for everyone, but at least look at things in light of God's word.

"Let's continue. Verses 11 through 19 describe a wealthy, productive, blessed, and rich land being lamented and mourned after its demise. Haven't we all heard America described as a rich land, a bountiful nation, a fruitful country? Is it possible that the description recorded in these verses could also apply to the USA?

"Then look at verse 20. The people of God are told to rejoice over her. Why would that be? Because, the answer reads, the apostles and prophets have been avenged. Although it might be a sad thing to see the land of our birth dealt with by a holy and just God, what would we rather have? Look how the modern-day prophets, preachers, evangelists, ministers, missionaries, and others have warned America of her decay. Then look at their treatment in return—scorned, mocked, and ridiculed. Look at the number of warnings, verbal and otherwise, that have been sounded. America seems to be plunging headfirst into hell, laughing as she does at the very ones who are crying out the warning.

"In all of this, in all our pastor was getting ready to tell us, in all that God has had me share with you, the one thing that still resounds from the precious pages of His written Word is that we should pray. Pray because we're told the fervent prayers of a righteous people avails much. Pray because all else is failing. Pray because if we do not entreat the Most High God for mercy, He may not intervene. Let's dedicate ourselves right now to praying for our nation as we never have before. As God assembles His people together, and it's obvious that's what He's doing. Let us pray that God's mercy might yet be extended one more time to America. Though we may not be able to change the heart, mind, will, or plan of God, it may be that He's waiting for our faithful prayers. He may be waiting to see if we desire mercy or judgment on our land. People, it's either prayer for mercy or apathy for judgment. And if you have purposed and set your will in agreement to pray for America, shall we not start right now? Let's make an altar of our pew and lift our voices in unison to the only true God who is capable of sparing our land."

Satan looked on in raging anger and disgust. He could tell Don had used God's inspired words to penetrate the hearts and spirits of those who had assembled there in one accord. He was powerless to do anything to so vast a number of unified prayer warriors. Hovering above the sanctuary roof was a dangerous place for him, and he knew it. Barely had Don made the request when the prayers of the faithful ascended like lightning bolts in reverse. Quickly dodging them, Satan blurted out, "Go ahead! Petition the Most High God. See if I care. I think I'll stir this murder thing up some more."

CHAPTER 12

Cimarron, Kansas

Dwight stepped back from the podium as he finished introducing Senator Harrison to the crowd of nearly four thousand supporters. It was a friendly and enthusiastic crowd, although there were a few hecklers scattered throughout the milling throng. There was even an occasional homemade sign that sported snide references to the Barton murder case. But for the vast majority, it was a joyful day of visitation by their candidate. A candidate, they were sure, who looked at life the way they did. A candidate who lived and stood for the same family values they stood for and wanted protected. Harrison represented that kind of candidate to them. And now, according to an apparent change of heart reflected by the pollster's own words, the "up-and-coming candidate to beat."

The point difference between candidates had dwindled in response to Harrison's surging popularity. The senator stood before the crowd with growing confidence, a mere ten points behind with only a few fading weeks to go before election day. Figuring in the three-and-a-half-point margin for error, that could easily equate to only a six-and-a-half-point deficit. Certainly not an insurmountable difference in light of the progress that had been made during the latter part of summer and early days of autumn.

Though the still-smoldering murder case in Topeka was not as much an election issue as it had been, from time to time it would flare up during questioning sessions with press. Some of the more hostile liberal reporters had continued to run their negative and nearly slanderous stories, intended more to increase lagging newsstand sales than to report factual news articles. The media types weren't the only ones encountering difficulty in trying to find something new in the nearly worn-out story. Police investigators had discovered that gleaning new clues were like finding meat on the sun-bleached bones of a dead west Kansas steer.

After the rally, Dick, Judy, and Dwight sat in their hotel suite making final plans in the schedule, drafting speeches, and discussing the upcoming week's strategies. Taking a short break from the session for coffee, Dwight picked up the front-page section of the local paper. The lead story covered in detail the rapidly vanishing point spread between Harrison's campaign and that of the opposition.

"That looks good," he said, displaying a large smile. At about the midway point through the article, the bold black type in parenthesis indicated a related story on page 3.

He quickly unfolded and opened the paper to the related article, only to find the headline Barton Murder Still Haunts Harrison.

"That's just great!" Dwight spoke out loud to no one in particular.

"What's the matter, Dwight?" Judy asked, looking inquisitively while pouring herself another cup of coffee.

Not being disrupted by the apparent start of conversation, the senator continued finalizing his next campaign speech.

"This news article upsets me! The Barton case still finds place in the papers even though it's been weeks since anything substantial or significantly new has been uncovered. Let me read this to you. 'Topeka Police Inspector Fritz Anthony relates there is very little chance of solving the Conrad Barton murder case before the fall election. His leads, to date, "are far and few between…fragmented pieces of data that don't seem to fit." Asked if he felt in his official investigative opinion there would eventually be a connection between the case and Senator Harrison's gubernatorial run, he related his opinion would be "only speculative, personal and not pertinent to the case, and certainly not appropriate for the press."

"'Investigation continues to center on the notepad found on Barton's body. Anthony did not reveal any new information on the contents of the notepad and has drawn criticism from other police

THE STATE OF CHRISTIANITY

agencies as well as the current state administration for not making full public disclosure of the details or contents of the notepad. Inspector Anthony did relate they are having a hard time deciphering many of the self-created codes and abbreviations the Barton notepad contained. "With no surviving family in this area, we're trying to work with a brother in New York. We hope to determine if the printing and handwriting are Barton's. Professional analysts are divided on its authenticity. Members of the denomination headquarters in Kansas City have been tight-lipped about Barton's employment with them. And the vast majority of the notations seem to deal in other presently nonrelated matters," Anthony said.

"'Anthony was asked if the heart of the notepad entries still involved the now famous "Rev Z math formula." To which he answered, "Without a doubt. It's the single most important clue we have to date." The formula, as reported to the media, was "Rev Z to be dismissed for supporting R. H. B. H. + inside + info = dead end."

"'"There are a lot of possibilities with that equation," Anthony disclosed. "Only the first two are fairly clear. *Rev Z* clearly refers to the reverend Donald Zigler. The reason we're so certain is that *Rev Z* was added after *Rev T* had been crossed out, an apparent last-minute change predicated on the sudden change of pastors when Pastor Jim Tomlinson had suffered his almost fatal heart attack. We're fairly confident that the *R. H.* is Senator Richard Harrison. What we can't figure out is who else was supposedly receiving Pastor Zigler's support, as the notation mentions. We haven't found a B. H. Nor do we know who or what the words inside or info refer to. It goes without saying, we're fairly confident the dead end was not supposed to refer to Barton."'"

"What else does the article say?" Judy questioned.

"It just goes on to say some things about Zigler and his church. It seems those who have attended his services say they're fairly normal except for Zigler's sermons, which are either dealing in politics or centering on the population increases in Kansas of late."

Dick quickly looked up from his writing, peering over the top of his half-lensed reading glasses to ask, "Do they say anything specific about the population increases, Dwight?" The senator was apparently piqued subliminally by the use of the word *population*.

"Oh, it's the same thing the police and the press keep asking about, that the church, or us, or both encouraged the radical fringe elements of your denomination to move here in order to gain some political strength through their voting. But the people moving to Kansas are from all different denominations and independent churches too. While the pollster's own figures show a large contingent of people switching to our side of the political and moral spectrum, I don't see how they draw us into that. And certainly no one, including us, has enough influence to pull people here from all over America as the story seems to suggest. Whatever the real reason for their move here is, it is true the vast majority are aligning themselves with our cause. One thing for sure, though, we don't have any particular group of voters in our vest pocket for election day. How I wish that were the case. I really think they're giving us credit for having more persuasive powers than we have. And they seem to think the general public is gullible enough to buy that hypothesis. They need to get out of la-la land and back to reality. If that were our purpose and ability, to persuade people to give up their established lives in other states just to join our cause here in Kansas, then think of the damage that would have on the conservative causes in those other states."

Dwight paused momentarily in his dialogue, evaluating what he had just said while displaying an intensely somber look. Soon a slight smile traced its way across his lips as though a pleasant thought had just hit him, then he continued his impromptu reply, "I'm astounded that they give us that much power or ability. They're certainly giving us credit for being smarter and more powerful than we are."

The senator slowly placed his pen back in his shirt pocket, set the pages of his speech on the table beside him, and looked Dwight square in the eyes, saying, "Dwight, I agree that kind of a scenario is pretty far-fetched for the human mind to conceive, let alone carry out. We must admit, however, something is happening here, something stranger than normal Kansas life. Or maybe a better way to say it would be something stranger than normal Kansas politics.

"Whatever it is, they're giving the credit to the wrong person. We started this thing at God's prompting, a dark horse nearly forty points behind. Not only our campaign, but nearly every conservative candidate from state senate to county coroner, seemed doomed to defeat. I suppose our unstated goal was to stir things up enough to at least hold our own in the congress. We knew my senate seat would be hotly contested, hoping and praying it wouldn't be lost. But it's not just the strong backing of the conservative contingent across this state that finally jelled. It's the added strength of an influx of born-again believers to the state who have turned the tide and dramatically improved our chances of victory. So who was the mastermind behind that kind of magnanimous people mover project? Who indeed! I believe you know the answer. I certainly do!

"But not only have we overcome the significant deficit in the polls, we've done it in spite of the blatantly antagonistic smear tactics somebody has been using. Somebody who seems to know how to cast disparaging shadows all over our campaign trail. Somebody who seems to know the inside and outside workings of this murder thing that's dogged us for so many months.

"Dwight, we're going to be in the governor's mansion soon. And praise God, we're going to have a majority in both houses. The song says it well: 'He didn't bring us this far to leave us.' We're not only going to win this election. We're going to get life in Kansas back where Kansans want it—peaceful, prosperous, productive, and in line with the Word of God. That's what we've been telling the people we'll do if elected, and by the grace of God, that's just what we'll do."

*****

Secluded and alone in a darkened basement office, the Source starts a one-sided conversation on the phone.

"Richardson's been arrested for suspicion of murder." Appearing somewhat distant in his voice, the Source continued cautiously speaking softly into the phone. "It was you who made the arrangements and gave the order. I'm not going to concern myself in whether you intended to kill him, or it just got bungled up. That's not important."

A lengthy pause transpired across the miles of phone lines.

"What's done is done! I know who hired you for that job. Don't think I'm as stupid as Richardson. I can see how these two separate, independent activities got all tangled up. It probably would have taken Richardson ages to trace your activities back to the denomination. He may never have. He's in jail because he's inept. Big-time college kid trying to scoop out the press. Thinks he's going to be the next big-time reporter capable of influencing the outcome of a governor's race with his journalistic skills. He botched it!" the Source screamed, then just as quickly returned to a subdued tone of voice.

"I just don't want his mess to get on me. Do you understand what I'm saying? Quite frankly I don't care if it's him, Zigler, Harrison, or all three that hangs for the murder. But I don't want Richardson spilling his guts about me. I'm too close to the top! That could be too costly!"

The Source sounded even more distant and remorseful, bordering on emotional as he continued, "Now listen! We've already been hurt too badly by all this ineptness. The Harrison camp isn't as good as it looks. It's just that we've not handled ourselves or our opportunities wisely. We're going to start cutting our losses now. I'll do what I can from my end. The way things look, we may have committed political suicide for what's left of this election. Had I known right from the start the extent that denomination was going to get involved, we might have better pooled our resources and more closely coordinated our efforts. Maybe when all this has blown over, I can find out what their purpose was. They weren't very clear to me in what they were doing. They may have made a preacher look bad, but their hopes of having it damage Harrison didn't work. It's too late now to regroup, but we do need to back off, cool off, and get our plans drawn up for two years from now."

Soon the voice at the other end of the conversation interrupted. "I don't mean to be abrupt, but if you've got work for me, I need to get busy with it. What do you want me to do for you?"

"If you get a clear chance, take Richardson out. But whatever you do, take him out cleanly. If you leave traces behind, you'll never operate another day in Kansas."

THE STATE OF CHRISTIANITY

"What if Richardson talks before I get to him?"
"Send me a bill. You know the address?"
"No, I don't!"
"Just send it in care of Leavenworth!"

*****

"I'll ask you one more time," Anthony sternly and tersely stated while kicking the leg of the chair Richardson sat on in an effort to emphasize his frustration. "Who do you know at the denomination headquarters?"

"And I'll tell you one more time, Inspector. No one! Now let me out of here."

Richardson turned to face his attorney and blatantly asked, "What the hell are you doing for me? You know I've got rights. Why aren't you protecting me?"

"He's asking you questions that pertain to the case. If he weren't, I'd pitch a fit for you. If you don't want to answer or you want a new attorney, just say so."

There was a lengthy pause. No one said anything else for several minutes. Richardson's forehead was dripping with sweat. Anthony loosened his necktie and undid the top button of his shirt. Then pointing with his finger at Jeff from across the room, he said, "I know you killed Barton. Your attorney knows you killed Barton. The press knows you killed Barton. In fact, they're even getting the front page of tomorrow's paper ready to say so. They've been trying to hang a preacher for Barton's murder, but now we all know you did it. So why don't you just fess up?"

"Why don't you fess up yourself? You got no real suspect, and you're trying to wrap it up any way you can. It just so happens you know it won't hang on me."

"Okay, Richardson. If you want to take the fall, it's your future, but just for me, answer one simple question. Who contacted you from the denomination headquarters?"

"No one. I'm telling you the truth. Listen. I admit, I had a fraudulent press pass. That's the only thing you can get me for. Big deal, what's that? A misdemeanor? But I didn't arrange any murder. I just wanted some facts for a writing assignment. You checked it out. If you know I'm telling the truth there, why won't you believe me in the rest?"

"Because my seventeen years on the Topeka Force won't let me. You're my link to some conspiracy activities in some mighty high places. If I can't get them, then I'll settle for you.

"Mr. Walters, I'm going to ask the KC Police to keep your client but only until tomorrow's arraignment. The judge will set bail, if any. Then I'll be there to tell the judge of the possible political connection and see if I can persuade him not to set any bail at all. I don't want your client to see daylight until he talks. I guess we're done now. After all, its past midnight."

Richardson hung his head while Anthony talked. He hadn't planned on any of this murder stuff. He was in it for the money and to possibly blackmail someone in the next state administration for a high paying job, an administration that, all of a sudden, didn't look much like it would be a winner in November. And if it didn't win, it wouldn't matter anyway. Jeff wouldn't be getting any appointment if he was in prison.

Why should I hang for them? he thought to himself. *They just might be able to prove enough of a connection with the Barton murder to send me up for homicide.*

"Wait a minute, Inspector," Jeff pleaded. "Maybe I can help. There's no sense in taking the rap for more than what I'm responsible for. If I help you, can you help me?"

"We don't make deals in Topeka."

"Yeah, but we're in Kansas City."

"Okay. Based on what you tell me, I'll ask them to go easy on you. Now what can you tell me?"

"I got a call late in February. I thought it was another part time investigation job. The guy at the other end told me to get ready for some exciting, rewarding work. He told me to get enrolled with the community college for journalism. That would be my cover. Then he told me to start following the Harrison campaign. He would supply me with a press pass. All he wanted me to do at first was to head up a meeting with five others he had selected, providing me with their names and phone numbers. You probably have their numbers if you've got my phone call history. These five others would eventually be my help to accomplish the assignment."

"What was the actual assignment?" Fritz asked.

"Research. In-depth research into Harrison—his money, his sex life, his religion, his childhood, or any other personal area where a skeleton might be. I passed these instructions, along with a thousand bucks, to each of the others at a meeting in the basement of a warehouse. They all agreed to do the work. Each knew who was in charge as far as our little group was concerned, but they didn't know who was in charge of the operation."

"So who was in charge of the operation?" Fritz asked, hoping desperately for a name.

"The Source."

"So who's the Source?"

"I can't say for sure, but I've got my suspicions."

"All right then, I'll settle for that. Who do you suspect?"

"I believe that it's Dwight Feld, Harrison's campaign manager."

Fritz couldn't believe his ears. He stopped his pacing, stood frozen in surprise. Richardson's words, reverberating in his head, made a shambles of his reasoning. His normally clear and orderly thought process now lay scattered on the floor of his mind. Somehow, in the disarray of his mental files, came credibility to the claim that Dwight was sabotaging his boss's campaign, but Fritz just couldn't figure why. Then just as quickly came an internal resistance to the unbelievable accusation Jeff was making.

"I thought we had a deal. You help me, and I'll try to help you. You're not really asking me to buy that, are you, Richardson? I mean you could have told me the president was behind it, or even the pope, but not Dwight Feld. What makes you think such a thing?"

"Just one thing—his voice."

"Why his voice?"

"You have to admit, Feld has a most unusual voice. I'd say he's more identifiable by his voice than by his face. I've talked on the phone many times to the Source, which was the only way he identified himself. One of the first things Dr. Hemstead, the old battle-ax, told us in the journalism class was to get the facts and then go with the hunches. I soon found myself following my first hunch. I started watching Feld more than Harrison at news conferences and speeches. You have to admit, I had opportunity to see him almost every day. I also heard him nearly every day, comparing his voice to that of the one on the phone. Believe me, they match! They match in more ways than one. Not only the tonal quality, but the verbal style as well. They both have the same vocabulary and use the same adages and such. I'd stake my life on it, as I may very well be doing. Feld and the Source are one and the same."

*****

Satan was ready to spit nails. "They just keep at it, thinking they'll figure it all out. The poor pathetic mental weaklings are just incapable of understanding who it is they're up against. But still, it grates me that they've figured out as much as they have. More distractions! I need to infuse more diversionary tactics, instill more confusion, make darker the path of their investigation, cover the truth and force a few more lies. And then there's Feld. He's neither as strong or as well-hidden as he once was, and I think he's starting to lose control. Either he straighten up, or I'll need to dispatch a few of my warriors of darkness to teach him a lesson."

Steady and unchecked growth of those darkening clouds continued. Hell's gloom over the other forty-nine states encouraged Satan. Only Kansas had become a menacing field, littered with the carcasses of one lost battle after another. Only Kansas was showing signs of overthrowing the forces of evil that had once been so firmly entrenched there. But all was not lost, not yet anyway. While victory was not yet assured to his satisfaction, Satan knew his stand here against the mounting rebellion would have to be one of undeniable power, force, and coercion, or it could lead to similar revolts in other states. Such revolts elsewhere would be entirely unacceptable—even the thought of it made him distraught. For generations, he had heard the saints talk of the "ultimate victory" belonging to the Lord God,

THE STATE OF CHRISTIANITY

but that was not going to start happening now, or ever, so long as he had anything to say about it. Times were getting difficult for him in Kansas, and the time had arrived for him to take a more active role in Harrison's defeat.

But what should that role be? Satan wondered. *Let me start with an evaluation of just how badly have things really gotten.*

CHAPTER 13

Topeka

"I certainly appreciate you allowing me to talk with you again Reverend Zigler," Tom Masters said, entering the rectory. Shaking hands, Tom continued, "After all that's happened this summer, you have every right to throw me out on my ears. I intended to call you several times to apologize for the way those stories showed up in print. I guess I never quite made the time for the apology. Please believe me, they didn't appear in the paper exactly as I wrote them. The news editor intercepted them on their way to the press computer. I think you would have found my draft copies a bit more congenial toward you and your precarious situation. But I didn't come here to make long teary-eyed apologies. I've come to share with you, things I've found out about the case."

"You mean all you've found hasn't gone into print?"

"No, I've held some things back, and if you'll give me an opportunity to regain your trust, I think you'll see you've been set up, a setup I started unraveling shortly after our last chat, but one that, in my estimation, won't stick. There is one thing, though, I may need you to confirm a few things for me as I go along. Are you willing, sir?"

"I've been advised by Police Inspector Fritz Anthony not to talk to anyone, especially the press, but you've certainly got my curiosity raised. For the time being, I'll at least listen to what you have to say. Go ahead, Tom."

"I know Inspector Anthony well. We have a good working relationship on case-related information. He's trusted me with informa-

THE STATE OF CHRISTIANITY

tion he has in exchange for some things I've found in my investigative routines. That's not a confidence I'm ready to jeopardize just for a jump on a story. If you trust him, call him and see if he will tell you that it's okay to talk to me."

"No, that's quite all right, Tom. Tell me what you know."

"Bear in mind, before I start, I don't have a great deal of tangible evidence to back this up yet, but should your case ever go to court, you'll find it comforting to know there are some, including me, who will testify to what I'm about to share with you. Over the past few months, I've discovered a handful of people who genuinely support your position and believe you to be innocent. I'm referring to people outside your congregation and inside denomination headquarters.

"I told Fritz the police keep attacking this murder case from the same old perspective, from the murder backwards. They should be doing what I did—get the motive and then go forward until you arrive at the murder scene."

"And just what was the motive?" Don cautiously asked.

"Silence, Pastor! To get silence! My guess is Barton knew something, something big and probably potent enough to control the outcome of a gubernatorial election, but he couldn't be trusted to keep his mouth shut any longer. That or he simply found out more than what he was supposed to."

"Can you share your suspicions with me?"

"Sure. As you know, Barton was employed at denomination headquarters. You told me that you hadn't seen or been introduced to anyone but clergy during your initial hearing, the hearing you told Fritz seemed to come off preplanned. He was there, though. You just couldn't see him. I snooped around and got a copy of the headquarters staff listing. Barton's name was on that list in two positions. One of the jobs listed him as assistant librarian for the main denominational library. That job doesn't seem to have any part in the case. The other job, however, maybe his recently gained main job, was as recording secretary. It was he who officially recorded the proceedings of activities such as your so-called hearing.

"The reason you didn't see him was because he was hooked up electronically to the proceedings. Barton was in his office keying in all that transpired during the session when you were suddenly notified of your dismissal. I found that out recently after slipping away from the group during one of their tours for the public. But remember when you expected the heavy questioning to start, the whole thing stopped rather abruptly?"

"Yes."

"That's because they already had your answers."

"Huh?"

"Yes, they had Barton key in a transcript with their questions along with what was supposedly your self-incriminating answers. Next, he did an actual transcription of the proceedings as you experienced them. Finally, the two were merged together, every now and then adding in your actual words to lend it some authenticity."

"I'm a bit confused. What did they say I said, and why?"

"I have to admit I was confused for a while too, but once I penetrated their security through a denomination insider, who, by the way, is on your side, it was evident that you were part of a manipulation to link you with Senator Harrison. A manipulation that was apparently scheduled to happen to over twenty other vocally active churches across Kansas. I suspect they were going to pick off each pastor quietly one by one from within the respective congregations, keeping the whole thing as low profile as possible. Only your case caused them problems right from the start. They had your pastor marked as first to go when his illness proved to be a godsend to them. With him out of the way under quite natural causes, they could, in turn, move on to the number 2 church. From here on, my words are, just my speculation, conjecture, at best, based on the many pieces of information Fritz and I have put together.

"Then things really got out of control when Barton was murdered. The contrived connection between you and the senator, I suspect, was meant to distort his character and make suspect his political motives for running for governor. This was probably the best they could hope for out of an otherwise deteriorating situation that was constantly being rethought as the unfolding situations called for. Who knows what they had intended if Barton hadn't turned up dead. I suspect if they could have discredited your stand from the pulpit well enough for a permanent removal, all the better. You were a pawn, an expendable one at that, but the main target they were gunning for was Harrison. If they could get you and the other potentially troublesome pastors out of their way by their efforts, their mission would have been a complete success. At any rate, I got copies of all three of those transcripts, which are probably the most damaging evidence to date to the denomination hierarchy. Inspector Anthony has them too, but you won't see that in the press. You see, my inside contact for information had recognized the fraud for what it was, knew it would come to a head someday, and was smart enough to make copies of those transcriptions before they became food for the paper shredder.

"Some of the questions they supposedly asked, and your answers went like this: 'Do you believe you should tell the people of your congregation how to vote?' Do you remember that question?"

"No, I don't because they didn't ask me that."

"I didn't think so, but you blatantly answered, 'Yes,' according to the transcript. 'Have you ever encouraged members of your congregation to be politically active or engage in civil disobedience?' was the next question they asked you."

"My goodness, that's certainly a loaded question. How did I answer it, or shouldn't I ask?"

"Of course, you answered, 'Yes.' The questions kept getting more and more specific. 'Who have you stated, to your congregation, should be the next governor?' You answered, 'Without a doubt Senator Harrison.' The questions continued by asking you if you would explain why you thought Harrison should be the next governor. You answered, 'Because I've learned that his hidden agenda would support several current issues I believe in that include tax increases on the lower-middle class, education reforms which would mandate government involvement in the selection of public school curriculum, provide for state funding of enforced secular day care, eliminate homeschooling, and eliminate parental consent for school authorities to dispense various forms of birth control to elementary through high school students.'"

"I said all those things, did I?"

"Yes, and then some. But you get the idea. It was a lengthy hearing, lasting well over three hours. Naturally all your very voluntary and incriminating answers easily confirmed to the hierarchy that the charges of politics from the pulpit against you were true."

"I can understand your confusion, Tom. Especially when the way I described that hearing to you, it couldn't have lasted more than fifteen to twenty minutes. You've really got me interested. Tell me what else you've discovered?"

"Frankly, Pastor, that wasn't the part that confused me. Although I was puzzled at what they were doing, more puzzling was why they were doing it and how much more they had planned to do. Or was it planning to do before the murder disrupted things and brought unwanted attention in their direction?

"Well, some of the other things I found out you might find interesting was that Barton was nearly the lowest-paid staff member. His salary edged out the janitorial staff for last place by only a few thousand dollars annually. My inquisitive mind immediately wondered if there was a possibility he might be experiencing financial difficulties.

"I estimated his rent, utilities, car payment, insurance, and food to be nearly three hundred dollars a month more than his gross. Even living alone as he was, in a lackluster apartment with no immediate family, he would have needed much more income than what I was able to determine he was legitimately taking home. I asked Fritz Anthony to get a court order and take me through Barton's apartment where we got into his financial papers. That's where we found a disparity. Instead of what you would assume, that he might be doing some moonlighting to supplement his income, the exact opposite was the case. His annual salary, divided by twenty-six biweekly paychecks and minus taxes, totaled more than his automatic deposit to the bank. With no obvious record of where the remainder of his salary was going, we dug deeper. His pay stubs and checkbook deposit entries matched, to the penny, the automatic deposit records from the bank. Thus, we had nothing to show where the rest of his income was going. Then we noticed a half sheet of paper, folded three times, and stuck behind his checkbook register. On it we found our answer.

Well, maybe *answer* is the wrong word. It was more like a rat's nest. It was a handwritten financial record of the past seven months. What it reflected was some regular cash deposits into another account. After each payday, an annotation reflecting a deposit was made in the amount of $92.30 in an apparently nonrelated business account in Kansas City. But all we had was this homemade ledger. Nowhere in his personal papers were there any deposit slips. We couldn't even find a purchase agreement or payment contract showing he owed that business any money.

"Now remember, I said he would have needed more money to live on, yet here was proof that some of what he should have been taking home was, excuse the cliché, vanishing into thin air, religiously being deposited elsewhere, and for no apparent reason, and in a very unorthodox manner.

"We didn't let the denomination payroll office know what we had learned, but Fritz, along with a KC Inspector and me tagging along, asked them to explain where the residual amount of Barton's pay was going. They pointed out that Barton was using the cafeteria on the payroll deduction plan. According to them, he had unlimited meals available to him in return for a flat rate withheld from his pay. They were quick to tell us Barton ate all three meals each day at the cafeteria. Silently, I wondered how they were so certain of that among employees totaling over three hundred, and when, during our visit to Barton's apartment, the pantry was so amply stocked. In fact, I'd say Barton was eating better than I do. They couldn't explain why the cafeteria deduction wasn't showing up on his pay stubs, adding they'd be sure to check into that. I had to admit, the dollar amounts they cited for the cafeteria deduction and the missing pay matched exactly. That didn't explain, however, why there was a lunch box in Barton's apartment, left there by him on the day he was murdered, a lunch box with a half-filled thermos of coffee, a candy bar wrapper, and one uneaten oatmeal cream pie. Like I said, a rat's nest.

"Does all of this point anywhere in particular, Tom?" Don asked.

"Not all by itself, not, at least, without the motive behind it. Fritz told me he had a hunch that Barton was being used by someone to leak the findings of your mock trial, along with possibly being a regular source of information on other denominational business. Now that would explain why he might be receiving extra income, if indeed he were, and may likewise be the reason he was found with so much money on his body. But conversely, it wouldn't explain why he was making regular deposits to an account that wasn't his with money that reportedly was paying for his meals, meals he shouldn't have needed if he were bringing a lunch to work. Nor does any of it explain why he would agree to rig your testimony, let alone how he was being compensated for doing so."

"It appears you have far more questions than answers," Pastor Don interjected.

"It looks that way. But the list of unanswered questions goes on. For instance, how, from whom, and why he had that large sum of money on him at his death is anyone's guess. All the crisscrossing of money simply had me baffled at this point. And what was being done with it could only be speculative, at best. Fritz said they still haven't determined whose money it was for sure.

"Well, getting back to the special account he was making roughly hundred-dollar deposits to every two weeks. We soon found out it had been receiving similar deposits from other employees as well as larger deposits from other unknown benefactors, and nearly all of it in untraceable cash. At the time, Inspector Anthony got authorization to look at that account, there was over $105,000 in it. Surprisingly, all the account activities, including the biweekly deposits, stopped right around the time Barton was murdered. That seemed strange to Fritz and I because of what we had gleaned from bank records that showed the previous history of regular, timely deposits. I just kept wishing someone would come forward and explain it to me. At that time, I could only speculate someone was trying to launder money in a most peculiar way. Apparently, they didn't have much knowledge of how to properly accomplish that task. Maybe making it look amateurish was their intention.

"That last idea intrigued me, so I pursued it. Sure enough, the Barton deposits, as well as the many other employee deposits, were going to a company by the name Data Files Inc., a bogus company,

THE STATE OF CHRISTIANITY

I found out, used to make political contributions to the opposition candidate for governor as well as other liberal candidates across the state. We had our connection even if we didn't have all the answers. It might take a while after the Fair Elections and Campaign authorities, or even a grand jury, start looking into it, but I bet they'll find a withdrawal equal to the amount found on Barton's body.

"Are you in any personal danger knowing all of that, Tom?"

"Oh, no doubt I am! I could easily be the next one lying dead outside a phone booth, just like poor old Barton. That doesn't scare me, though, now that I have a somewhat better idea of what's going on. I didn't for the longest time, which I hope explains my crudeness at first. Something was out there stinking, so I just kept digging. My gut feeling is that sooner or later, the one behind all of this is going to be revealed. And, Pastor, do you have any idea who that person might be?"

"No! Who?"

"The owner of that bogus company, Data Files Inc., Dwight Feld, Harrison's campaign manager!"

"Are you serious?"

"Quite! That tidbit of speculation could, if true, cost me my life, but I think it's just the tip of a political conspiracy iceberg."

Don scratched his head and looked as though he were deep in thought. Then standing to his feet he said, "You know something, Tom? Inspector Anthony said basically that same thing. He mentioned a possible conspiracy some time back in his early investigation. It seems the two of you are onto the same thing."

"Well, sir, we are, and we aren't."

"Can you explain that little paradox?"

"Sure. You see we've had occasion to talk and compare notes. He and I agree on the possibility of a politically motivated conspiracy, but we differ on our hypothesis. He seems to think it's origin—the conspiracy, that is—is strictly in the political arena."

"And you, Tom?" Don pressed.

"I believe it's a denominational thing."

"I think you just lost me. While I agree Senator Harrison is a member of our denomination and that he actively supports many of the church's positions on the moral issues, why would the denomination plan and execute anything that could or would preclude his election?"

Tom smiled widely, stood, and zipped up his jacket. "When you get the answer to that question, you will have several options to consider."

"I suspect you're playing a game with me now. Don't you dare keep me guessing! You know the answer to that question, don't you? And just what do you mean about my 'several options'?"

"No, I haven't got an answer yet, but I have my suspicions. But if you can answer that question before I do, you can join the staff at the *News* as an investigative reporter, or you can run for chief of police, or..."

"Or?"

Tom turned to leave while talking back over his shoulder, "Or you can apply for the job of head position of your denomination."

"Wait a minute, don't leave me on that note. I've got one big unanswered question left."

"What's that, Reverend?"

"At the beginning of this conversation, you mentioned Barton knew something big enough to affect the outcome of the gubernatorial election. I would assume you meant the election was being manipulated in such a way as to ensure Senator Harrison wouldn't get elected. In light of the eroding lead of the opposition candidate, I'd say whatever it is, or was, is just a moot point now and probably has been nearly all along. Just what does that do to your deductive reasoning? After all, Harrison's chances are actually growing better every day."

"Bingo! What you hold in your thought process right now is the key to unraveling it. What if Inspector Fritz and I are both right? What if the conspiracy is twofold? What if they are or were two distinct, autonomous conspiracies, unknown to each other at the outset of Harrison's gubernatorial bid but joining forces just prior to the murder? What if one of those conspiracies was tapping Barton for information and paying him for it, while the other was blackmailing him for money because they knew what he was doing? What if the two conspiracies discovered each other after getting tangled up unintentionally? And then, unknown to Barton, joined forces against him? Or it may very well be that the only one who knew there were two plots was Barton himself. That knowledge could have been the reason for his demise. I'm grabbing at straws as you can tell. Any or all of those ideas could be right, or none of them. It nearly boggles the mind, doesn't it, Reverend?"

"I'll say. But Barton wouldn't have been the only one who knew. Whoever it was that knew, Barton knew also. And lest we forget, God knew. Do you think there's any chance that all of this will get figured out and take the suspicious heat off the senator and me?"

"If there's any hope of that, it lies with Inspector Anthony, the KC Police, and may require some help from your friend upstairs."

Don smiled, lifted his eyes to the heavens, and said, "To be sure, the Lord will deliver. He's been doing that right from the beginning of time. But as for my thoughts on what you've said tonight: wow! You've simply astounded me. What in the world has this nation come to, Tom? Tell me, do we have any remaining hope for our society without first incurring the wrath of the Creator?"

Tom turned once again to start his departure. "I think you're asking the wrong man. All I can say from this twisted situation is that strange things have been happening in Kansas, and only a handful of people know the truth of them. God help us! I believe only those of you with some kind of special spiritual insight can see these happenings for what they are. But to me they seem like some kind of unseen evil force on the prowl, setting its hook and attempting to pull down America!"

"Tom, the fact that you can make that kind of assessment leads me to ask if you're a child of the King?"

"I really don't know how to answer that. My knowledge of religion is very limited. I do believe there's a God, and He will ultimately be revealed. Whether I'm a child of the King, as you put it, is something I can't say."

"If you have a few more minutes, Tom, I'd like to help you make an evaluation of your spiritual state."

*****

"This is getting entirely out of hand! Each time I set that preacher up for a fall, he turns to that mess at Calvary and takes another one out of my hands. What's he trying to do anyway? Doesn't he know he can't save all the world's lost by himself? I've got to stop his momentum and snatch the victory out of the jaws of what looks like certain defeat. Just what tactic shall I employ this time? Something that will catch even God by surprise. I know! I'll let Feld take the fall. That will appease them! And then, while they're all basking in the momentary triumph, I'll finish the job. America will be fully mine. From DC to the West Coast. America, my springboard to the world. We'll see whose garden it really is! I haven't forgotten that 'crawl on your belly' thing. He may have placed man in charge over all the earth, but I'll be the one telling man how to do it."

CHAPTER 14

Kansas City

Inspector Anthony sat poised for action in front of the handcuffed Richardson, fighting the tiredness he felt and that was displayed on his face. Although he had slept periodically during the past several weeks, his sleep was not restful because his mind had continued to echo question after unanswered question. Every clue that had been painstakingly uncovered only revealed the need for more clues to resolve the escalating mystery. For now, though, he would force himself to be as alert and ready for this important session as he could be. He had even splashed cold water on his face in the restroom across the hall from the interrogation room. He was hoping Richardson would be able to provide answers to those countless gnawing questions that had been piling up over the past several months. Fritz felt almost certain the information Richardson would soon be providing would be significant to him and the Kansas City Police. Information that would undoubtedly aid them in moving closer to reconstructing the seemingly endless chain of events. This was even in spite of how insignificant it might appear coming from the part-time, small-time operator Richardson obviously was.

Richardson's attorney was present, sitting beside him while impatiently loosening his tie, then unscrewing lead from his expensive-looking mechanical pencil. Because Fritz and Tom Masters had become friends over the past several weeks, he allowed Tom to be present as well during the questioning. Jeff knew he had to tell the truth if he even hoped of getting out of jail. He was certain that those present would smell a lie or cover-up from a half mile away.

"Okay, Inspector, I'm ready to begin. What did you find out about dropping the murder charge against me?" Jeff nervously asked, pausing from his habitual nail-biting long enough to get the question out.

"The KC Police and I have discussed that," Fritz answered. "Everything is really in your hands. It will go much easier on you if what you relate helps us in wrapping this thing up. Do you understand there are no promises?"

"Yes, I understand that. I just thought maybe you had something a bit more tangible than that. What do you want first?"

"Just start at the beginning as you know it, then we'll ask any questions that you don't answer with your statements."

"Okay. Let's see. Shortly after the first of the year, I received a letter which offered to hire me as an investigator. That wasn't all that strange. I get job offers nearly every week. Most come from jealous husbands or boyfriends wanting me to check up on their wives or girlfriends, not necessarily in that order. I'm not a licensed private eye, but I can do what they do for a lot less money. And besides, I like the work. The letter used the phrase 'fact finder for a political action committee.' Of course, I had done that kind of work from time to time too. Sometimes doing things a little shady or illegal, things legitimate private eyes or PAC workers couldn't run the risk of doing. The jobs usually paid me fairly well. I guess you could call me a freelancer.

"But getting back to the letter. It went on to inform me of where and when I was to meet with someone. The initial meeting would be in a week, at which time more specific instructions would be given. I went to the place the letter specified, a small cafe in Troy. Once there, I met a fellow who sat next to me and asked if I was looking for work with a political action committee. I told him I was. He didn't identify himself but claimed to be a representative of his boss, the Source. He handed me a package of starter materials, as he called it, and told me to go home, study them carefully, and call the number given at the time specified to verify my acceptance of the assignment.

"The package was a large brown envelope containing a letter of instructions, a list of names and phone numbers, a fake press pass, a key, an itinerary of Senator Harrison's campaign schedule for the upcoming week as well as some of his long-range plans, and lastly, well, almost lastly, a phone number where I should call. The last thing was eight thousand dollars!

"After counting the money, I started reading the letter. It told me to contact the men whose names appeared on the list provided and set up a meeting with them in a specified warehouse basement."

"Do you remember the name of that warehouse?"

"Yes, Data Files Inc., north, a little ways, of Topeka. That's what the key was for. I was told to make the meeting look like a poker game. During this meeting, I was to inform the men of what we were to do and to give each one who accepted the assignment one thousand dollars to get them started. Each of us, myself included, was to snoop around, looking for anything we could find about Senator Harrison that might be of value, anything that might be hyped up or exaggerated and cause the Senator to be less appealing to the voters. We were instructed to find as many skeletons in Harrison's past as we could. In fact, if we didn't find any, we were expected to create them.

"While most of the instructions were for all six of us, there were also some specific instructions for me. I was required to enroll in a community college course in journalism. This, coupled with the fake press pass, would be my primary cover. I was also to disburse the money to the men who accepted the assignment—all five of them did. I would later receive and disburse additional money they were to receive as their work progressed. However, my most important job was to work my way into the campaign press corps and follow the senator, checking in from time to time with the Source, while doing my own digging as well. I was the only one who received weekly pay. Good pay, I might add. The others received money sporadically. I think since January there wasn't a week that I didn't receive at least five hundred dollars cash, plus expenses and a rental car. Can you see why I was intent on keeping this going?

"The men would check in with me from time to time with little more than an apology for finding nothing. Although they were all working independently, they shared in the lack of results. You have to remember Senator Harrison is a good man. In all of this, I've learned that. There simply wasn't anything we could find that even gave the appearance of impropriety. I started feeling pressure to produce something, but the money kept coming with little more than a bawling out by the Source, and even that came over the phone. Eventually he had me fire the other five.

"His paranoia soon became evident as the lead for governor eroded. He started screaming at me because the lead was shrinking, and I hadn't found anything on Harrison to injure his character or personality. He told me to look deep into the area of state population and voter registration. He seemed to think Harrison was somehow underhandedly attracting people, primarily conservative Christians, to Kansas long enough to be legally registered voters, get him into office. And then, at some time after the election, they would eventually return to their home states. That plot seemed just too far-fetched an idea for me to believe, yet I was getting paid pretty well and enjoying the work, so I followed his strong suggestion. He supplied me with the name of a person in the Bureau of Stats and Analysis who would provide me with the information necessary to substantiate his theory. Obviously, my job would be to fabricate the story and spread it in casual talk among the other reporters, hoping that sooner or later it would show up in somebody's news story. That was the purpose for that package of data I received when you arrested me."

"That's it?" Fritz questioned.

"Yes. I never got to see the statistics or to verify or repudiate his theory."

Fritz leaned forward in his chair, rubbed his eyes momentarily, and then asked, "So tell me again. Who's the Source?"

"Like I said earlier, I believe it's Dwight Feld. At first, I didn't know who it was. It wasn't until I started following the senator that my curiosity got roused. Then while at my first or second press conference, I made the connection. He came out from a side room, jumped up on the platform, and started talking, preparing the press corps and then eventually introducing the senator. Right from the first word he spoke, I knew his voice sounded familiar. Although the telephone can distort some voices, not his. In practically no time, I was certain I knew who he was. Naturally I never let on that I had figured that voice out. I had taken my original instructions from the owner of that unique voice as the Source. Even though I can't prove it, I'm certain it's Dwight Feld."

"Did he ever say anything about why he was working against the man who employed him as a campaign manager?"

"No. And I didn't ask any questions. I didn't want to jeopardize the money flow or my lifestyle. He didn't know I knew, at least I never confronted him. The money was too good, the job too exciting, and the opportunity too important to me. You see, I was planning ahead to after the fall election. I was planning to use what I already knew to secure a cushy job in the next administration somewhere. If I let on that I knew who he was, I could probably kiss any potential job goodbye."

Fritz stood to his feet, tugging at the knot in his tie. "This may be the most important question I'll ask you tonight. What you've told us here, would you testify to these things in court?"

"Yes, if it means you drop the murder charge."

"Let me ask you one thing about that. Are you sure you don't know anything about Barton?"

"I know he's dead. That's it!"

"Okay. Now I'm satisfied. Officer, get the release in order for his attorney. Then I think it's time to visit two other people—Bishop Hammond and Mr. Dwight Feld."

*****

Bishop Hammond's lavishly appointed office was on the top floor of a three-story building, situated on a secluded and densely wooded parcel of the nearly one-hundred-acre site. It was separated from the rest of denominational offices, yet connected by an underground walkway roughly a half mile long. While the day-to-day work of the offices was accomplished in a large new five-story glass-and-steel structure, the bishop's offices were in the recently remodeled original headquarters building. Stately in appearance and dating back to the late 1840s, the architecture and decor could easily impress heads of state from any nation in the world. Outside the stately oak trees and vivid floral arrangements would excite any botanist. Inside, room after room, including the wide hallways, had been meticulously appointed with works of art ranging from ancient Chinese and Egyptian pottery to priceless paintings from every corner of the world. Even the floor covering was modern-made replicas of carpeting from those pre-civil war days.

Inspector Anthony, several Kansas City policemen and a sheriff's deputy approached Bishop Hammond's office, stopping in front of his secretary's desk. Fritz did the speaking, offering his badge for viewing as he did so.

"We're here to talk to Bishop Hammond. Is he in?"

"Yes, he is, but he's in conference right now," the attractive young lady, identified as Mary Forrester by the nameplate on her desk, answered. "Would you mind waiting over there? His conference is nearly finished. If you'd like, help yourself to a cup of coffee."

"Thank you, Ms. Forrester."

All the men except Fritz sat patiently in the plush cushioned chairs at the opposite end of the reception area. He strolled the perimeter of the room, looking at everything that could be looked at, wondering to himself where to start his questioning once in the bishop's office. He continued to stroll around the room, studying the pictures on the walls, then the brochures in the information display, and finally the large family-type Bible on the coffee table. He opened the Bible to see if the dedication page had been completed. It had.

"Excuse me, Ms. Forrester. Could I ask you a question?"

"Why certainly, sir. It's down the hallway to the left. Third door on the left."

"No, no, that's not what I was going to ask. The dedication page on this rather expensive-looking Bible says, 'Dedicated to the many hardworking people of denomination headquarters upon my inauguration into church hierarchy, this fourteenth day of March in the year of our Lord, nineteen hundred seventy-five. Signed B. H.' Could you tell me who B. H. is?"

"Of course. That's Bishop Hammond. He very often initials things that way and, as a result, is affectionately referred to as B. H."

THE STATE OF CHRISTIANITY

As he sat down to ponder the equation found in Barton's notebook, Fritz felt in his bones he had another missing part. He started mentally kicking himself for looking at Bishop Hammond as Fred Hammond all these many months. He got out his pad and pen, quickly rewriting the formula: "Rev Z to be dismissed for supporting R. H. B. H. + inside + info = dead end."

Fritz assembled his suspicions in his mind that *Rev Z* was Reverend Donald Zigler. *R. H.* was, of course, Richard Harrison. And if *B. H.* was Bishop Fred Hammond, all that remained was to find out what "inside + info = dead end" meant.

A faint buzz was heard as it came over the intercom system, alerting Ms. Forrester that Bishop Hammond was now out of conference and available. Standing from her desk, she announced that she could now usher them in to meet the bishop. Once they were all inside and seated, Bishop Hammond entered through a nearly hidden side door.

"Gentlemen, it's good to see you. I hope your visit here is for pleasant purposes. Is there anything new on the Barton murder case?"

"We thought we had the right suspect when we arrested Jeff Richardson," Inspector Anthony started, extending his hand for the bishop's as he did. "But we just couldn't find enough evidence to hold up. We had to let him go. We'll continue to watch him, though." Fritz wanted to ease into the driver's seat of the conversation very cautiously and carefully. Word selection here would be critical. He searched the bishop's face for clues as he spoke, but found none.

Continuing, Fritz asked, "We encountered several things about Mr. Barton's finances that, quite frankly, we haven't been able to get any satisfactory answers to from your payroll office."

"Would you like me to get someone from that department over here?" Bishop Hammond interrupted, reaching for the phone, ready to make the call.

"No, that won't be necessary. It's really not that big a deal right now. You see, they told us he was using the cafeteria payroll deduction plan for all of his meals, yet it wasn't showing up on his pay stubs. That's probably just a fluke or a glitch in the computer program. Would you agree with that assessment?"

"Sure sounds good to me," the bishop responded, smiling widely as he did. "You know how computers are, right? And besides, I don't get too involved in the minutia of that side of administration."

"Tell me, Bishop, would you say Barton was a loyal employee?"

"I have to presume he was. He had over twenty years with us here at headquarters and before that, clerical work at a small church in Richfield. That's in the southwest corner of the state. I believe, having looked at his personnel records shortly after his murder, there wasn't anything derogatory in there. My opinion is, he was just a steady, honest, God-fearing man."

"Well, sir, maybe there was nothing at work that would cause you to question his character, but honest, law-abiding citizens are not normally beaten to death outside phone booths with thousands of dollars on their person."

The bishop fidgeted slightly, then looking concerned, asked, "I'll leave that to your expertise. Do you have some kind of conclusion for what befell Mr. Barton? After all, it has been several months now, and this is your first visit to our offices in a long time."

"We believe he was being paid to divulge information about denominational concerns or activities. We don't hear of big news stories coming from your headquarters very often, but is there or was there anything big on the agenda about the time of Barton's death?"

"Let me see if I can recall anything in particular." First, the bishop scratched his head, trying desperately to look like he was thinking, and then fumbled through his one-year calendar pad on his desk. "I can't imagine anything important enough to get paid for or get killed over. The biggest thing going on in our denomination this year is the rapid increase in church rolls. You know, praise God, it really looks like there's revival going on out there."

"Why do you say that it 'looks like'? I would think you would know for sure."

"Just a figure of speech, Inspector. Let me say it this way. There's revival going on out there across Kansas! Praise God again!"

"Do you know that, or are you basing that strictly on the figures?"

"Well, figures don't lie. We depend on them all the time. But this year they've been telling us that church attendance is up, Sunday school enrollment is up, congregational membership has moved upward, and naturally the collections have been up too."

Fritz motioned to one of the other officers while saying, "Make a note of that. That sounds like something that may need to be looked into, at a later date." Returning his attention to the bishop, he asked, "What do you attribute all of that to?"

Suddenly Bishop Hammond became impatient and went on the defensive. "Inspector, I just got done saying it is because of the revival going on here in Kansas. That's just the way church business should be. What's your concern? Why are you asking me these questions? They don't seem relevant. Why did you come here today?"

"Frankly, Bishop, we're very close to cracking this case, and we just need to have all the little minute pieces necessary to weld it all together. It's common knowledge and has been in all the major papers that Barton was found with a notebook that showed a possible connection between Senator Harrison and Reverend Donald Zigler. We know the main duty Barton performed here was as recording secretary and, as such, was involved in the Zigler hearing several months back. Do you remember that incident?"

"Yes, I certainly do. Pastor Zigler was charged with and found guilty of politics from the pulpit. We here at headquarters were appalled. After a very lengthy and extensive investigation, we dismissed him. His church appealed. Now it's pending review. No big news story there now, though, just internal church business. It might have been news a few months back, as I recollect. My, how time flies, doesn't it?"

"Yes, it does, Bishop. And I'll agree that for a while it was something the press was following, but apparently someone was more than interested in the connection for its news value, and Barton seemed to be in a position to know what was going on. Have you ever seen this before, Bishop?"

Fritz slowly placed photostatic copies of the three transcriptions in front of the bishop, while never allowing his eyes to lose contact with Hammond's face.

"I recognize one of these as the official transcript of Zigler's hearing. I don't know what these other two are. Tell me, how did you get them?"

Fritz didn't answer. He just pressed the bishop harder. "Look again, Bishop. Each of them is a transcript of that hearing, but only one of them is real. The other two are fraudulent. We're having trouble determining which one is the actual transcript. Would you please examine them again, carefully, to identify the true one?"

With sweat starting to surface on the bishop's forehead, he reviewed each of the three documents, doing so in such a manner as to appear to be complying with Fritz's request.

"This one is the true transcription," the bishop responded after several minutes. "I really don't know what these other two are, but maybe they're excerpts—that's it! They must be excerpts."

"Nice try, Bishop. Here's the real transcript!" Fritz tersely stated while pointing to the actual record of the event. "You know that too. You know about the $92.30 biweekly deduction from Barton's pay and the pay of many other employees here. I have a hunch you know about the $105,000 political action fund, and you know that Barton and others were making coerced contributions to that fund by making deposits into an account in the name of Data Files Inc. These deposits were probably the only means he had of keeping his job. No doubt if he missed making a deposit, he'd be gone like a tumbleweed in west Kansas during a microburst!"

"Inspector, I resent these accusations you're making. I think it's time for you and these other gentlemen to leave."

"I don't think so, not yet anyway."

"I could call security."

"Call whoever you like. We can carry this conversation on downtown. Would you feel more comfortable there?"

There was no answer.

"I suspect you know who was telling him to leak that information to the press as the threat of being unemployed forced him into more and more dirty work for the denomination you head. And you know who ordered Barton's beating—I presume it wasn't to kill him. While you might feel Barton was a loyal employee, it might very well be that that loyalty was costing him $92.30 per payday. He knew that you and the other puppets on the board were originally planning to trump up falsehoods against Pastor Tomlinson, changing to Zigler when Tomlinson was taken out by the unexpected heart attack. All your contrived innuendoes in Zigler's case were to be leaked by Barton to the press in hopes of soiling Senator Harrison's reputation.

"No doubt he eventually reasoned, very accurately under the circumstances, the Lord taketh and the Lord giveth, that, of course, being a different twist on an old saying. Denomination was taking money from him, so he took information from the denomination, more information than what you told him, selling it for whatever he could get for it. That probably didn't amount to too much until just before his death. Somebody got to him with some cash—big cash. Not $92 in payroll deduction but big-time income. As you said, there wasn't much happening here of importance. But once he knew what you were doing to Zigler and why, he found himself in a moneymaking situation, a situation that turned a political ambush into a murder.

"Another thing, Bishop, the political platform of Senator Harrison, while in line with the spiritual dictates of the church membership at large, would not be beneficial to you and others in power positions within the denomination. You, for instance, have had the ear of the past two governors and now the current one. While you have given the appearance of keeping church and state separate, it's common knowledge that you are often called upon at times to add validity or lend support to many of the social programs being cranked out by his administration. You liked the notoriety. They liked the pseudocredence your moniker and presence provided. That powerful status simply had to be continued into the next administration no matter what the cost. With the right people making that known to the political higher-ups and Harrison's reputation and character blemished beyond repair, you could be assured of that happening. Yes, to be sure, Harrison is a member of your denomination, but the fact of the matter is that he stood for change, change that threatened your power base and would leave you on the outside looking in. You see, Bishop Hammond, you're much more guilty of politics from this pristine palace than Zigler is from his humble homilies. While Harrison and Zigler stood for morals and truth, you fell for power and influence.

"Once you could see the handwriting on the wall—that is, Harrison's election chances getting better and better as time progressed—you intended to turn up the heat. But before you got a plan drawn up, Barton switched allegiances. You see, I suspect you did what all of us did for the longest time—that is, assume you were the only people who didn't want Harrison elected. Events show us someone else was playing in your game, and neither of you knew it. Their proposal to Barton with its money was too good an offer for one poor old man to refuse. When he wasn't following your orders as quick as you thought he should, you decided teach him a lesson in loyalty. You had someone beat him up. They overdid it, though. Didn't they, Bishop?"

Again, there was no answer.

"Okay then, don't answer. I'll continue. I've got this confession all ready for you to sign when I'm finished. Do you know what the minimum sentence is for murder, Bishop?"

A somber Hammond leaned forward in his chair, holding his face in his hands, shaking his head yes. "But you haven't got all the pieces, nor do you have them in the right order. Your suspicions are only partly correct. Don't stop yet, Inspector. Keep digging. You'll see it when you talk to Feld. Don't think so small."

"Officer, you can take the bishop downtown and book him, but skip the cuffs. He'll go peacefully."

Satan went screaming off into his own darkness, "Nooo!"

CHAPTER 15

Eureka, Kansas

"And as we enter the final days before the election, the people of Kansas prepare to make their voices heard. The odds were against us from the start, but we didn't concern ourselves with the odds then, and we certainly don't concern ourselves with them now. We have, however, always tried to concern ourselves with telling Kansans the truth while making sure we are cognizant of the needs, hopes, and will of the people. During this campaign, I have been intent on exposing what's wrong and expounding what's right in this state—what's right for the people of Kansas and what's right for the government of Kansas. As of today, there are only three points between us and the opposition, who, at one time, led by nearly forty points. We're becoming more and more confident each day, yet we caution you to not think the election's already been won. Nor do we want you to get complacent, thinking it won't matter if you stay away from the crowded polling places. The fact that a high-voter turnout is expected only increases the need for you to be dedicated to the cause, that being to return Kansas to sanity and responsiveness. Remember this also, you must vote for those other candidates who will support our platform and who are determined to govern the people according to the wishes of their constituents.

"For Judy and I, let me take a final moment before I close to thank you for turning out in such large numbers to greet us on our swing through your town. It's going to be in towns just like Eureka, where the election will be won or lost. Stand by us, vote, and watch our beloved Kansas as it shows America the way back to the basics of democracy, back to the foundations of freedom, and back to its once held pinnacle of greatness. Thank you very much. May God bless you richly."

The crowd started to disperse amid cheers and the resounding strains of patriotic music played by the Eureka Senior High School band as it marched down Main Street and back to the campus. Senator Harrison, Judy, along with Dwight and several other dignitaries, retreated to the nearby hotel restaurant for a civic luncheon. Inspector Anthony greeted the senator as he entered the dining room amid the secret service and local police escorts.

"Hi, Inspector. I don't believe I've seen you for better than two weeks. Are you still on the trail?" The senator spoke softly, quizzing Fritz while shaking his extended hand.

"Yes, I'm still hard at it. And you're right. It's been two weeks exactly. I guess you could say I got diverted. Listen, if it's not going to be a problem, may I borrow your campaign manager for a while this afternoon?"

"Whatever for?"

"I believe he has some information I'll need to get from him if I'm ever going to wrap this thing up. But I don't want to disrupt your plans."

"Well, sure, Fritz. I can manage by myself this afternoon. Judy and I were going to spend the time just relaxing here in Eureka while visiting with some friends up in our suite. As soon as the luncheon is done, you can have Dwight, but please get him back before our strategy meeting at 8:00 p.m. if you can."

"Thank you, Senator. We shouldn't keep him that long...Then again, we might."

The sudden and startling noise of Dwight straightening the gooseneck microphone in front of the crowded banquet room brought the conversation to an abrupt stop. Senator Harrison wrapped one arm around Judy and the other around Fritz, saying, "Come on, Fritz, have lunch with us on the dais."

"I'd like that, sir, if it doesn't put anyone out."

THE STATE OF CHRISTIANITY

"No. I'll tell the waitress to set another plate. Here, you sit on this side of Judy."

*****

"Dwight, let's make this as pleasant as possible for everyone concerned. We need to ask you some very serious and pointed questions, and we don't want a PR man's song and dance. We want the truth."

Dwight's brows furrowed, then he asked, "Why in the world would you preface your questions with those statements, Inspector?"

"The reason why doesn't really matter," Fritz continued. "What can you tell me about the opposition candidate? You know, the stuff that doesn't get printed."

"Please excuse me, Inspector, but aren't you asking the wrong side? I don't mean to answer your question with a question, but what you want is something the opposition's campaign manager can answer, not me."

"Well, I suppose you're right based on the way I asked it. Let me rephrase the question then. How would you describe the opposition candidate?"

"An oaf, an incompetent. He hasn't done a thing with all the golden opportunities he's had in this campaign. He could have dusted our britches more times than I care to count. He could have and should have had a field day with us. I guess the same thing holds true of his campaign manager—incompetent, that is. Yet through all the missed opportunities, he has clung tenaciously to his ever-decreasing lead. He hasn't employed even the slightest of smear tactics. I would have expected at least that much from him. Maybe he's trying to offset Senator Harrison's personal faith and character with his own case of 'saintly' behavior. Why do you ask?"

"Well, to be honest, Dwight, we've run into a diversionary venue in our investigation of the Barton murder."

"You mean you're still seriously working that one? I assumed that case would have gone out with the trash by now. I'm impressed, Inspector. You guys must be doing a pretty thorough job."

"You might not be so impressed when I tell you about the diversion and how it got us distracted—distracted, that is, until we put many of the fragmented pieces together."

"How so?"

"I'm glad you asked. Our investigation kept looking at things from a political perspective, yet everything we came up with pointed to unrelated areas, including a personal vendetta. Tom Masters of the *KC News* wanted to compare notes with me, kind of a mutual-sharing-of-information agreement we had going. He seemed to think a religious motive was involved, with the senator being a born-again Christian. I had my doubts about that aspect. After all, who more than the church would want one of their own in the governor's mansion?

"Masters and I laid the whole thing out end to end, so to speak. His journalistic investigating seemed to validate my side, and our findings seem to validate his theory. The reason neither of us was getting anywhere was because we were both right and didn't know it. Strangely, we seemed to be getting the pieces from two different puzzles mixed up. You ever try to do that, Dwight?"

"Not intentionally, no."

"That's what brings us here to Eureka. We figured if we could talk to you in detail about the political side of things, then we might be able to wrap the investigation up this week. Wouldn't that be nice. A knockout punch right before the election. You know, clearing the senator's name and some of that ugly press that's been out there, dogging him throughout the campaign. You do believe that would be the thing most likely to put the senator into the governor's mansion, don't you?"

Dwight slowly settled down into a plush leather armchair, lowered his head a bit, then quickly corrected his outward appearance to fit the feigned response he hurriedly formulated in his head.

"Why, of course! It would be just what we were hoping for at just the right time, but does that mean you've got the murderer?"

"We don't have the actual person or persons who beat Barton up, if that's what you mean. With what we do have, though, we can show the prosecutor back in Topeka that a serious conspiracy existed on two separate fronts and that one was religiously motivated and the other, politically."

"Have you got any names at all?"

"Several. Yesterday we booked a high official at the denomination headquarters where Barton worked."

"Well, that's good. Have you made a public announcement on that for the papers to pick up?"

"Not yet!"

"Well, for the senator's sake, why not?"

"Because if we had, we'd have jeopardize the political side of our investigation."

"Oh, I see, that's where I come in, right? That's why you're here. To get information on politics?"

"You could say that. Does the name Jeff Richardson mean anything to you at all?"

Fear gripped Dwight as he returned to the chair. Trying to control his emotions, he said, "Let me think. It does have a strangely familiar ring to it."

After a pause of nearly thirty seconds, he responded, "Ahh yes! I remember where I've seen that name. Richardson's in the press corps, or was for a while anyway. I think he's dropped out for some reason or another. He was crisscrossing the state with us for a long time. I don't think he's been on the trail of late, and I can't recall what news agency he represented. After a while, all those press passes look alike from a distance. Certainly, you're not saying a member of the press corps was in on the murder?"

"No, not the actual murder, but part of one of the conspiracies. What else do you know about him?"

"Nothing else really. What part did he have in the conspiracy?"

"He's really small potatoes, but he's fingered some pretty big-named and unnamed people. And here's the funny part, Dwight—he's named you!"

Silence dropped in the room like a bomb. Dwight seemed visibly shaken before he could gather his composure.

"My word, what does he say that would involve me in a murder?"

"I'm not at liberty to answer that, Dwight. What can you tell me about Barton?"

"Nothing more than what the papers have reported."

"Come on, Dwight, think really hard. I believe you know more than that. Hadn't Barton been supplying you with needed information about the senator's affiliation with a preacher in Topeka? Leaking it to you before he leaked it to the press?"

"No! And I don't like where your line of questioning is leading. I think you'd better leave now!"

"We're not leaving, Dwight, and you know it! Not until we get what we came for. Would you like to go somewhere else less comfortable to answer these questions?"

Again, Dwight slumped down in the armchair, drooped his head momentarily, and then went to tapping his fingers on the arm of the chair. He shook his head no, then paused to look directly at Fritz, asking, "Just what do you know about me?"

"Dwight, we've got a whole lot of implications. You might be the senator's campaign manager, but I believe in my guts you're working for the other side. My guess is you were putting out as much bad publicity about the senator as you were the good stuff—maybe even more. I believe Barton's inside information on the church's investigation into the Reverend Donald Zigler of Topeka was important to you. However, I also think it was just the tip of the smear-tactics iceberg. You were no doubt paying Barton for the information, but maybe he started getting greedy. Maybe he started getting antsy to get out of a near-poverty lifestyle, take a long vacation, or maybe he wanted a big new car. Regrettably, he's not here to tell us. Maybe he started asking you for protection. Maybe something else altogether. Until you tell us, we might not know. That is, until your court date. Now tell me this, did you give the order to have him beat up?"

Dwight stood slowly from the chair, walking to the window, and looked out without saying a word. Then, with face red and slowly rubbing his hands in a nervous methodical fashion, as if applying hand cream, he replied, "I suppose that's what the bishop told you. It was really a joint decision. Beat up? Yes! Murdered? No! The boys did too good a job. That wasn't what we told them to do. You have to believe me. I knew when I started double-crossing the senator, trying to sabotage his campaign from within, that sooner or later I might be caught. I also knew that even if I didn't get caught and by some miracle, as the senator would call it, he got elected, my best place would be right in the mansion with him. If I couldn't cause his defeat in the campaign, maybe I could cause his failure as governor and get him out after just one term. The bishop called it plan B or 'getting inside.' In retrospect, I guess you could call it a suicide mission. It was something I just had to do. I believe the senator's political agenda will be most disruptive in the state. He had to be stopped before he had an opportunity to undo all the reforms that were in place. When Barton's murder hit the paper, I figured I would be the last place the police would look for the responsible party. I kept up the act while the bishop and I kept our distance, something we agreed upon right from the start. That way, if one or the other fell, the momentum wouldn't come to a complete stop. But with Barton killed instead of just taught a lesson, I had to go back and start covering my tracks, and that seemed to boomerang on me. You see, it looked good on paper. Just get everyone to think it was political. Then throw in enough of the religious stuff to get everyone confused. I had the contacts, the bishop had the power, and Barton and Richardson were the disposable little men. By the way, you better start protecting Richardson if you haven't already started doing so. He's got a paid contract on his head."

"Don't worry, Richardson's safe. So you knew the bishop's involvement, the bishop knew yours, and you both knew Richardson and Barton's involvement. I just assumed they were two distinct conspiracies."

Fritz sat down for a moment, thinking about Barton's formula. Retrieving his notebook from his jacket, he started rewriting it with explanations he muttered out loud. "We know *Rev Z* equals *Reverend Zigler*. He was supporting R. H., and that stands for *Richard Harrison*. B. H. equals *Bishop Hammond*. And according to what you just said about plan B or 'Inside,' that explains that part of the formula. 'Info,' I assume, means what Barton had access to in denomination headquarters or maybe about denomination headquarters. Information that he hoped meant money, big money. Lastly, if Barton got his big money, he could finally leave his otherwise 'dead end' job. Regrettably, the only dead end was Barton's life. That means the only thing missing from the formula was you, Dwight. There's no *D. F.* in the formula. Maybe you were an after-the-fact part of Barton's intention. Sure. By the time you entered his life, he had already written the formula. He was working both sides against the middle and wound up the loser.

"So then tell me, Dwight, do you know who the Source is?"

"You mean you don't?"

"You can confirm our suspicions. He's the missing part. We're still looking for him."

"Well, you can quit looking. You've just found him!"

*****

The lights in the large tent had been burning late every night for the past two weeks. Volunteer church workers had assembled the tent and a temporary platform from which Brother Domi could preach. They had carefully dismantled and brought with them the pulpit all the way from New Orleans. In fact, it was the only part of the old church that made the trip other than the hymn books and nearly three hundred believers from Faith Community Fellowship.

The land, just outside of Hutchinson, on the northern edge of the city limits, had recently been purchased. Plans, site preparations as well as actual construction were well underway on a permanent prefabricated building that would be ready by Christmas. At first, many of the families felt out of place so far away from their home, but life had moved on, and everyone had lent their strength in helping each other get settled into their new environment.

Brother Domi checked the sound system and shook his head approvingly after a quick "test, test…one, two, three…praise the Lord!" followed by a loud hallelujah. In just a couple of hours, the fellowship of believers would begin, and Domi would be sure to point out the delivering hand of God in the events of the past five months. Most of the congregation wouldn't need the reminder, though. They had seen God's move firsthand. They had been a part of His end-time move. They had experienced something they had never experienced before. For them, all that was left was the shouting.

In Winfield, Pastor Billy McPherson's flock had merged with an already established church that had relocated from Ethelsville, Alabama. They too had been called by God, heard that call, and been obedient to it. With the addition of the Holy Ghost Baptist Assembly from Detroit, their ranks had nearly doubled. Dr. and Mrs. Jiles had met Winfield's need for a physician in the small community where Mrs. Jiles sister, Charlene, lived.

At their first combined service, Ethel was asked to play the organ, which hadn't been touched since the loss of Saint Winifred Chambers, who went home to be with the Lord nearly three months ago. Now Ethel felt at home, playing those hymns of her childhood and bringing the congregation to their feet in praise and worship to their God. Pastor Billy smiled as he watched his wife's face glow with joy. As she continued to play, he mentally retraced their recent journey, stopping from time to time to thank the Lord for His faithfulness and demonstrated power to deliver.

Pastor Howard Schmidt and Assistant Pastor John Simms led the rest of the congregation in procession through the new sanctuary. Although much smaller than what they had in San Francisco, the new facility met their needs adequately. Though they had long ago surrendered their formal church liturgy, they had retained and were now using the Davidic practice of parading with banners and celebrating spontaneously before their God. Their move had been costly in terms of riches left behind, but those losses paled into insignificance when compared to the might and power God had used to propel them from the West Coast. All the legal problems had been overcome, and liquidating church property had been rushed through the administrative process by people who seemed quite happy to have the church closed. Pastor Schmidt had compared their exodus to that of the Hebrew nation. God had given them a pillar of cloud by day and a pillar of fire by night. The pillar of cloud seemed to shelter them from the heat of the evil one that pursued them, while the pillar of fire gave them a sense of light which illuminated their direction to Kansas.

Emporia just seemed like the right place for Reverend Ted Arsley's church from New York to settle. It was country yet close enough for them to get to Topeka or Kansas City if they felt the need for a refresher course in big city congestion. They knew their work in Kansas would be different than back in the Big Apple, but only after the initial two tasks were accomplished. Obviously, one task was to get settled. The other was to become familiar with and join the fight against abortion in their new homeland. Both tasks were nearly accomplished with the blessing of God going before them, preparing the way for many successes. Reverend Ted hadn't changed his style at all as he kept hammering away at the arguments of the pro-choicers. He had been given a verse of scripture on the way-out west that became his trademark: Proverbs 28:2, "For the transgression of a land many are the princes thereof: but by a man of understanding and knowledge the state thereof shall be prolonged."[20] He and his congregation accepted with eagerness the call to come to Kansas and with equal enthusiasm greeted the call to arms, declaring the message of God to the people.

Larry Gillespie embraced Pastor Stanley Sharp's wife and welcomed her to his new church in Independence. Quickly she answered his obvious question and pointed out her husband, who stood talking to some others of Larry's church on the other side of the fellowship hall. Larry excused himself and walked immediately to Pastor Sharp's side. He couldn't believe their paths had crossed again. They shook hands and chatted about how God had finalized all that he had shown them that Wednesday night back in Atlanta.

Larry's Pastor Baily along with Pastor Sharp, who had now been joined by his wife, started to share with others in the social gathering their future plans for the two neighboring churches. Everyone seemed in agreement, in one accord as the second chapter of Acts puts it, when they heard the many upcoming events that would be the joint venture of these two autonomous bodies of believers, events that would help shape the outcome of the upcoming election on both state and local levels. Things like voter registration blitzes, plat-

THE STATE OF CHRISTIANITY

form discussions, informational forums, as well as driving pools for assisting voters to the polls. Things that would have been frowned upon in earlier days when the term separation of church and state had been twisted and distorted into something it wasn't meant to be.

Larry sat with his wife, holding her hand, intently listening to all that was being said and formulated. Nothing could jar his concentration from what so intently captivated him—nothing, that is, except for a strange yet comfortable inner feeling or nudging to turn and greet the person who had just sat down in the folding chair next to him. As he did, his eyes met those of a beautiful black woman—Roxanne. His prayer had moved a mountain. The Holy Ghost had kept an appointment. The blood of Jesus had reached her. Now saved, she was a part of God's family from Atlanta, and as such, a part, too, of this mighty move. They looked at each other, momentarily in a daze of near unbelief, then both broke into tears, not tears of sadness or joy but at utter amazement at the precision of God's powerful plan.

CHAPTER 16

Topeka

"We open our newscast this evening with the latest breaking events in the seven-month-old Conrad Barton murder case. Police today announced the arrest of several persons believed to be involved in not only the murder, but who allegedly were involved in at least two separate conspiracies, conspiracies reportedly directed at discrediting the gubernatorial campaign as well as the personal and public character of Senator Richard F. Harrison.

"The first arrest, that of Bishop Fred Hammond, most high bishop of denomination headquarters in Kansas City, took the clergy from across the nation and the religious world in general by surprise. The full involvement of Bishop Hammond in the conspiracy and murder has not been released by authorities at this time, due in part to the sensitivity of the continuing investigation. Reliable sources also related that the bishop was providing extremely critical information, but whether he was just being cooperative with authorities or hoping to work a plea-bargaining deal was not disclosed. Details were also sketchy on the arrest and suspected involvement of two low-level workers in the schemes. Arrested and indicted on conspiracy charges was Jeff Richardson, originally from Elkhart, Kansas, now living at a Kansas City address, and Jack Philips, a data collection and entry clerk at the Bureau of Stats and Analysis here in Topeka.

"Richardson, a former member of the junior press corps who was following the Harrison campaign, was supposedly working under the cover of political reporting assignments from the Kansas City State Community College, where he was enrolled. Philips's involvement in the alleged plot was not stipulated. However, we have confirmation from an unnamed source inside police headquarters in Topeka that Philips was merely providing statistical information from the wealth of data maintained in the state office where he worked.

"The biggest news release surprise of the day, however, came when the special investigating officer from the Topeka Police, Inspector Fritz Anthony, revealed during a late afternoon's press conference that Senator Harrison's own campaign manager, Dwight Feld, had been arrested. Official details are scarce at this time, but Inspector Anthony said the roll Feld played in the murder would be pivotal to the prosecution's case and could not be made public at this time.

"Senator Harrison was not available for comment or interview when our reporter, Brad Garmano, on the campaign trail contacted his campaign office. The senator's wife, Judy, serving as his interim campaign manager, made available this short statement, and I quote: 'While the senator is astonished at the recent turn of events resulting from the police investigation and regrets the arrest of his trusted aide and confidant, Mr. Dwight Feld, he feels he must not get diverted from his goal of being elected governor. Nothing has changed, no matter who has been involved in attacking the senator's reputation. The needs of this state and its citizenry is foremost in his mind.'

"In a related news story, we have this item just in. Though certainly not influenced by today's revelations, the results of the last pre-election poll were released and reflected a lead by Senator Harrison over his contender for the first time since the race began. The poll, which is subject to a three-and-a-half- to five-point variance, shows Senator Harrison winning next Tuesday's election by just short of seven points. Whether this lead will be influenced positively or negatively on the election results remains to be seen.

"In other news tonight..."

Judy, standing by her husband's side in the hotel room, leaned down to lower the volume on the TV. She paused momentarily, searching the grimacing expression on his face as he slowly rubbed his chin, obviously evaluating the report and its potential impact on

Tuesday's election. She could tell he was deep in thought, appearing almost trancelike.

Trying not to startle him, she softly asked, "Would you just as soon I turn it off altogether?"

"Yes, dear, I think so. It's time to think and evaluate what's transpired today. You know, take a good hard look at next Tuesday and what we do till then in light of all this activity."

"Let's pray first, honey, before we evaluate," Judy whispered, looping her arm through his. "Let's ask God to clear things up for us and get them into His perspective, not ours. Satan's handiwork is coming apart at the seams, so let's give God an opportunity to confirm once again His will to us and bless us with the peace of Christ. His delivering right arm of justice and power will be all we need to lean on and depend upon."

"That's why you're my interim campaign manager, dear, and probably should have been all along. You always keep a cool head. I agree. Let's pray."

*****

"People, I would like to close this Sunday evening service with just a few words about Tuesday," Pastor Zigler announced after the altar call was concluded and those accepting Christ were being escorted to a prayer room. "We've come a long way in the past year. We've encountered some of Satan's strongest onslaughts. His attacks have come from outside the church and, regrettably, inside. We've been slandered personally and persecuted as the church of Jesus Christ corporately. We praise God for finding us worthy to suffer persecution for our Lord's name. Like the apostle Paul, we have 'fought the good fight, [I] we have finished the course, [I] we have kept the faith: there is, therefore, laid up for [me] us a crown of righteousness, which the Lord, the righteous judge, shall give [me] us at that day; and not [me] us only, but unto all them also that love His appearing.'[21] And if I may add, those who have come so far, giving up so much, leaving so much behind, and taking the challenge to start anew at the prompting of the Holy Spirit. Those of us who have stayed put to receive our brothers and sisters from across the nation had the easy part. All of us have been brought together 'for just such a time as this,'[22] so let's not be found slack in the hour of calling that approaches.

"There is another dawn coming, a dawn before the Son of God splits the eastern sky. That dawn is Tuesday, and while it does not promise to be the last dawn, it very well could be the dawn of the last opportunity for this state, should we be found unfaithful. This is not a time for doubt. This is not a time for unbelief. This is a time for signs and wonders to begin unfolding in our midst, in view of all Kansans. Indeed, in view of all Americans. We're too close to quit now. Be sure to do your patriotic duty on Tuesday.

"You know we're not just reaching out for a voting machine lever, but rather we're voting to shape the future of Kansas and eventually this nation. Consider your vote on Tuesday an absentee ballot for those"—Don paused to steady his quivering chin and wipe a tear tracing its way down from his eye—"those children who silently call on us to save their lives."

*****

The senator and his wife were up early on Monday morning, finishing their light breakfast of coffee, juice, and cheese Danish. Judy lovingly picked a small piece of lint from her husband's suit coat, smiling as she thought of the next several weeks back home in Concordia. The senator paced the floor as he gave his morning speech a final oral reading. As he neared the end of it, she moved in close and hugged him, lightly placing a kiss on his cheek. She held the embrace long enough to savor the fresh aroma of the cologne he wore. The loving way she held him broke his concentration. He stopped long enough to whisper a private word to her, causing her smile to widen momentarily.

Soon they were heading out of their suite for the elevator, preceded by bodyguards and followed by a sea of reporters. With their every step came the flashing and clicking of cameras amid the din of reporter's questions. Judy smiled and waved. The senator responded to only one question soliciting his feelings on being called governor.

"Sounds like what I've been called to do, what I've had in mind all along!"

*****

Monday morning's sun shone brightly and reflected off the side of the Topeka Trade, Industry and Agriculture Center building. The massive glass, granite, and steel structure, shaped like a pyramid, consumed three entire blocks of choice real estate and rose to a pinnacle twenty stories high, dwarfing most of the downtown buildings. The cool morning breeze was moderated by the warmth of the reflected sun. If tomorrow's weather was equally as fine, a large turnout of voters could be expected. Several thousand Harrison supporters had arrived and assembled in front of the TTIAC Building. Blemishing the otherwise picture-perfect setting was the small spattering of hecklers and unfriendly signs which touted the carrier's opposing points of view.

November was here. The campaign was nearly completed. This one final speech remained for Senator Harrison to make, here in Topeka, and then he and Judy were driving back to their home in Concordia to await the returns.

Judy stepped confidently to the mike. "Ladies and gentlemen of Topeka, I introduce to you my husband and the next governor of the state of Kansas, Richard F. Harrison."

Confidently he stepped to the microphone. "Greetings! It's looking good, isn't it?" the senator asked the crowd as he started his remarks. The people cheered and waved their signs and banners in response to the question. "Judy and I are about to head home for a few weeks of rest. It's been a rough ten months since we started traveling the width and breadth of Kansas, especially at the pace we've been doing it, but we wouldn't change a thing. That travel has confirmed and reconfirmed our purpose. It has also clarified our goal—to be the governor of the people of Kansas, not just the governor of Kansas. This stop wraps up the official campaign. The voters, that's you, tell us tomorrow who you want as governor and how you want the future of this State to be charted...

"And in the final analysis, any candidate must not only promise to govern by the will of the people but, if elected, keep that promise above all else. To sum up not only this campaign but the results of having closely checked the pulse of the people of Kansas, we know this course is sure. We know this course is sound. This course we have charted is in agreement with what you've told us it should be. Judy and I appreciate all the support and encouragement you have given us. We thank you for this resounding send-off back to Concordia. We also know that you will be here to receive us in January as the first family of our beloved Kansas. Thank you and may God bless you and your families richly."

The couple waved to the crowd, left the platform, and were escorted back to their suite.

It was nearly 3:00 a. m. Wednesday before the major networks declared Harrison the winner. The liberal element that controlled the visual media had tenaciously and stingily clung all night to the claim it was too close to call. But in Kansas City, the *K-C Gazette/Herald* front-page headline had already proclaimed it with one-inch letters: HARRISON VICTORY HEADS STATEWIDE PARTY SWEEP!"

In quiet bedrooms, on living room floors, and in prayer closets in virtually every town in Kansas, God's people were kneeling. Prayers were being offered in cars as they traveled along the highways as well as in spontaneous church meetings all across the state. Hundreds of thousands of prayers of thanksgiving were going up in unison. A spiritual commonwealth of communication that included praise unto the one true victorious God, who had once again shown Himself faithful. A living God who had rallied to their request, delighted in their defense, and who had miraculously visited His people, faithful to the good work He had begun and would continue to perform until the day of Jesus Christ.

CHAPTER 17

Topeka
At a news conference several months later

"Governor Harrison, sir, it appears, by the polls taken to date, that you are riding the crest of very high popularity with the people of Kansas. The fact that your victory was by only a few thousand votes, to what do you owe this surge of popularity in so short a time?"

Smiling widely, the governor responded, "If we are indeed increasing in popularity, it must be for many reasons, and none more than that the people are getting what they wanted—a rarity in politics anywhere these days. First, the election is behind us now. The people always like that, you know, getting things back into some kind of order and knowing the government has returned to the business of running the state. And, too, the murder and conspiracy trials have been completed. That's allowed the truth to come to the surface, where the public can view it and see the ugliness and fire that political aspirations can sometimes trigger when fueled or ignited by a hunger for power. Then there's the fact that we're rapidly dismantling the humanistic and socialistic bureaucracy that's been in place for so long, draining the financial resources and bogging us down in red tape and ineffectiveness.

"But I would be amiss if I didn't acknowledge another reason for the surge in popularity. Before I do, though, let me say I'm not concerned about popularity as it applies to me. I was elected to do a job. The people told us to do certain things, and we're busy doing them. If we have enjoyed some measure of popularity thus far, it's because of that and the fact that God has been merciful to our state, blessing it with many quick successes.

"The first thing we dismantled, a mere four hours after inauguration, was the abortion-on-demand laws. All through the campaign, the vast majority of people I heard were demanding an end to the murder. We've ended it! Though we accomplished that with a temporary measure sure to be tested in the State Supreme Court, the murders have been stopped. Even though it's for the time being, until we can get a more permanent measure in place, the people like that, and God likes that. When science, and in particular medical science, catches up and proves to its own satisfaction that life starts at conception, then the battle might be over. Until then, though, I'll fight for the unborn with all the strength I have.

"The second thing was to initiate the end of the state lottery. For years we've been told by psychologists that gambling can be addictive. If gambling can become addictive and, as they call it, a disease, then we need to get a cure for it. That cure, in my estimation, is to outlaw it. We should take the same measures against it you would against cancer—attack it with every known weapon and from every direction possible until it's defeated. We certainly didn't need to encourage gambling nor foster the social damage that comes hand in hand with a lottery.

"The third area we challenged was that of pornography. There are just too many documented police cases that painfully demonstrated and proved the direct correlation between crimes against women and children and the use of pornography. If there were that much evidence showing apples were the cause of common colds, they'd be off the store shelves by noon. The fact of the matter is, no matter how pornography is viewed, be it art or freedom of expression or the filth I believe it to be, it whittles away at the community decency and eventually becomes an ugly blight on the landscape. It's a trigger mechanism for acts of violence, and Kansas can do better without it. We're getting rid of it in Kansas!

"Can you see how addressing and overcoming one problem area strengthened the resolve of the people and the government to rid the state of others? Each success spawned and encouraged yet another. As we drew closer to God and His laws, as a people, the victories became easier and easier to overcome bad human laws. I suppose the way we got the way we were was because the opposite is true as well. The farther away from God we get, the easier the enemy infiltrates and the easier each defeat comes.

"Well, I know this is a lengthy answer, but we haven't gotten rid of everything yet. We still need to address prostitution, drugs, alcohol, law and order, and probably a hundred other issues that have pulled Kansas into the mire in years gone by. But if we are faithful to the pledges we made the people, if God continues to smile on us and our course of action, with His mercy for a little while longer, we shall indeed correct the vast majority of them. If we, as a people, are faithful to employ the wisdom God has so graciously provided, our efforts will be rewarded with successes that stagger our present-day imagination. Then with the rest of America watching, we will experience proof positive that our course is right. The blessing of God will make Kansas greater than she has ever been. You watch. That's not a politician's promise or some pie-in-the-sky hope. I found that in the Bible, 2 Chronicles 7, to be exact."

"Senator—excuse me, I mean Governor, what will be your plan for replacing finances lost from some of these so-called vices?"

"Thank you for asking that. We've already started addressing that issue. We would be errant to think that the primary source of revenues came from the lottery. Contrary to popular belief, that didn't constitute a major part of our income. Taxes historically have been, and will continue to be, the main source of revenue. However, we don't anticipate raising personal income taxes, nor do we want to raise the sales tax. The fact is, middle-income families have always borne the brunt of tax increases, and we don't want that to happen again. Even if we increase taxes on business, that just gets passed along to the consumer, and the middle-income families pay again with higher consumer prices. When families pay, they usually pay out of their budget, not from some hidden family surplus. The truth also reveals that there aren't enough wealthy folks to make up the loss if we increased their tax. All that might do is drive them and their current tax payments away.

"What we need is a new form of revenue that will not affect the Kansas resident. In other words, get the rest of America to finance our needs. I hope I've piqued your interest?

"There are a number of plans under review by my staff and me. The one that looks the most likely to work was a part of my campaign platform, although the others being studied may also be enacted. Every adult citizen will be provided a Kansas Resident Card. This card, unlike a Social Security Card, will be a means not of taxation but of avoiding increased taxation. Residents, by showing their KRC card, will continue to pay sales tax, income tax, and all other user fees at the current rate. Outsiders, however, those operating vehicles, doing business, earning money in this state but living elsewhere, will pay taxes and user fees at a higher rate. Should they decide to locate their residence here to benefit from the lower taxes and user fees of a resident, then they are welcomed, and we're none the worse off for having gained a full-fledged taxpayer. If they elect to travel through or make their money here and leave, they can do that too, but it will cost them more, more to use the highways, more to buy gasoline, more to purchase food, clothing, a night in a motel, operate a business, or whatever. Colleges and universities across the country have been successfully employing this policy for years in computing tuition rates, so we know it's constitutional. And the nation as a whole can ill afford to avoid us. Our productivity and contribution to the GNP is a vital part of the nation and its commerce. They ante up or do without. I know Americans. They'll not do without what Kansas has to offer!"

"Sir, what are some of the other ways of increasing revenues that you're looking at?"

"It's just too early to say right now. We want to think this one through all the way first. If you take on too many at once, they have a tendency to get muddled and blurry. Suffice it to say, we're moving cautiously and with precision in this extremely important area. Whatever we eventually enact, we want to view its potential effects on each segment of our society. The one thing we don't want is to accidentally hurt anyone with legislation put on the books too rapidly. What we do want to do is to encourage, stimulate, and benefit from an economic environment far surpassing anything previously experienced in Kansas or the nation. If we can do that, and I believe we can, then ours will be an example to the rest of the nation that I feel is in very serious trouble. Now I think I had better close this news conference. I appreciate you're being here today."

Over three years later

The governor readied himself for a few token campaign speeches and appearances in his bid for reelection. There was no real opposition. No one, except a few who were determined to remain locked in Satan's blindness, would even dare speak negatively of the successes and record of Governor Harrison's first term. It was all there in black-and-white. No one could argue with the facts. Kansas had prospered phenomenally. Crime had been significantly reduced. Drugs had been virtually eliminated from schools and nearly eliminated from all other places, including the inner cities. The homeless were being cared for by a model program that was being studied by Washington and copied in several large cities in other states. Prostitution and the resultant arrests were reduced by almost two-thirds. Pornography had returned to its place of hiding, openly and blatantly showing its decadence nowhere in prominence for over two and a half years. Alcohol consumption was declining voluntarily.

In other areas, productivity of the state had nearly doubled, attributed primarily to new lines of food products. Three farming seasons in succession had culminated in increased production, while the neighboring states were suffering from reduced yields. As a result, prices for farm commodities soared, with Kansas reaping a swelling monetary harvest as well.

Beef production also rose, resulting in new state records being established. The unrivaled success allowed the industry to benefit from several world trade deals. The state coffers were swelling from the revenue measures introduced by Governor Harrison as well as increased receipts from higher personal incomes. Sales of durable goods statewide were brisk, contributing to a higher influx of sales tax revenues. The ever-increasing state population was adding thousands

THE STATE OF CHRISTIANITY

of tax-paying citizens to the rolls. The economic, social, and health picture for Kansas was growing brighter every day. Unemployment, which had soared to over ten percent prior to the Harrison reforms, had declined to nominal levels, bringing the state's prosperity to nearly every household. Income tax reduction measures were being introduced before the legislature. Nearly every financial expectation of the Harrison administration had been met or surpassed.

Success stories from Kansas were showing up almost daily in magazines, newspapers, and on the evening newscasts across the nation. Representatives from Kansas had moved into pivotal and prestigious positions in the federal government as their wisdom and influence were sought by those of other depressed states seeking solutions to their chaos and turmoil. Truly, the rest of the nation was sitting on the edge of its seat, watching with great interest the blessing of God that was blanketing Kansas and its people.

The spiritual condition of Kansas continued to improve as well, reaping a bountiful harvest of souls in unprecedented proportions. Sunday nights across Kansas proved it. Services hadn't been the same for years. Most people who used to stay home on Sunday nights watching television were now attending every service, and the churches statewide were filling up. Such was the case in Pastor Zigler's now independent congregation. Previous to this mighty move of God, morning services were full, but Sunday nights had been attended only by remnant believers. Not so anymore. Now people weren't showing up just to take a place on a pew. They were coming to pray and learn of God's power and majesty. Their desire to praise and worship Him could not be constrained nor denied. And too, they were coming to see more of His signs and wonders. They came early to pray before service. They were praying during the service and praying after service. They were even praying at home and on their jobs. Pastor Zigler had instructed them well, and the Holy Spirit was leading and guiding a growing army of prayer warriors.

The significant thing was that Don's congregation was not alone in the intense prayer. It was almost as if Someone had written a letter of instruction to every church across the state. The larger denominational churches had come out of the scandal purified.

What could be shaken had been shaken so that what couldn't be shaken could remain. They were all stronger, more viable churches—the small independent as well as the storefront community, the black gospel church in the inner city, the way-out-in-the-boonies rancher's church, and the large and small from north, south, east, and west. In each of them, people were putting their knees on the floor and calling out to God for mercy, forgiveness, blessing, and hope. The people were tearing down Satan's strongholds and claiming the victory of their God. In a word, revival—no, in two words: true revival!

People who hadn't seen the inside of a church in years not only were there regularly but enjoyed being there. They wanted to be a part of God's outpouring Spirit in this latter day. By the power of the Holy Spirit, their eyes had been opened. They could now see the spiritual pollution that had nearly overtaken their state. And that was still making a high bid for the rest of the nation—all but Kansas, that is. Satan's plan was finished there! And he knew it!

Satan was being dealt a deadening blow, and God was using Kansas to do it, just like in Topeka many decades earlier, during the early 1900s. Back then God had used the state of Kansas as a springboard for His Holy Spirit to sweep westward to Azusa Street in Los Angeles, California. Then in 1906, His Spirit-led revival rushed eastward back across the entire nation. Once before, He had started revealing and demonstrating His power from this central point in America, and now He was doing it again.

Once before, a remnant people of God had grown weary in their struggle for holiness and for a oneness with God. Once before, a peculiar people, a royal priesthood of believers, had tired in their desire to remain pure in the midst of a nation that was locked in the decadence and immorality of the preceding gay nineties. And now He had another assembly of believers ready to receive from His Spirit.

Once before, a small but readied remnant of a generation had heard, seen, and experienced firsthand the one true God shake their land. Once before, with humble and obedient believers from humble and sanctified places in Kansas, God had started touching the hearts, minds, and spirits of a people, not just any people but His people, a

THE STATE OF CHRISTIANITY

people His Son had gained for Him. From Kansas, God had started a national Pentecost in America, just as He had in Jerusalem when the day of Pentecost had fully come.

Now once again, a wind was blowing. Once again, *the wind* was blowing. This time, the effects would be bigger. This time, its start would get the attention of more than a few preachers and a handful of believers. This time, it would gain the attention of believers and nonbelievers alike! This time! Yes, this time, it would usher in the harvest time of His work in America and the world! This time! This time, it would ready a worldwide family of believers for His Son's return! This time, praise God, it would change forever the state of Christianity!

THE END

NOTES

Chapter 1

[1] Matthew 18:20 (NKJV).
[2] John 6:60 (KJV).
[3] Romans 1:28–32 (NKJV).
[4] 2 Peter 3:10 (NKJV).

Chapter 2

[5] 1 Peter 2:9 (NIV).

Chapter 3

[6] Isaiah 35:1–10 (NKJV).
[7] 1 John 4:4 (NKJV).

Chapter 4

[8] Mark 10:14 (NIV).
[9] Philippians 2:15 (KJV).

Chapter 5

[10] 1 Peter 2:9 (NKJV).
[11] 1 Peter 2:9 (KJV).

Chapter 7

[12] Joshua 24:15 (NKJV).

Chapter 9

[13] Jeremiah 51:1–10 (GNB/TEV).
[14] Jeremiah 51:13 (GNB/TEV).
[15] Jeremiah 51:8 (KJV).

Chapter 11

[16] Matthew 10:23 (KJV).
[17] Revelation 18:2 (KJV).
[18] Revelation 18:3 (KJV).
[19] Revelation 18:4 (KJV).

Chapter 15

[20] Proverbs 28:2 (KJV).

Chapter 16

[21] 2 Timothy 2:7–8 (KJV).
[22] Esther 4:14 (NRSV).

ABOUT THE AUTHOR

Dennis Beaudry, originally from Monroe, Michigan, is a retired Air Force master sergeant who served as a personnel specialist, technical instructor, historian, and career advisor during his twenty-six-year military service career. After retiring, he was employed with The Ohio State University in various data entry positions. He married hometown sweetheart, Linda, and has two adult children and four grandchildren. He resides in Columbus, Ohio.

CPSIA information can be obtained
at www.ICGtesting.com
Printed in the USA
JSHW021556110423
40200JS00001B/13

9 798885 407205